W0017954

CONTENTS

BEST
LOVE
LETTERS
OF
ALL
TIME

CLASSICS

Published 2024

FiNGERPRINT! CLASSICS
Prakash Books

Fingerprint Publishing
@FingerprintP
@fingerprintpublishingbooks
www.fingerprintpublishing.com

ISBN: 978 93 8993 113 6

L ove . . . It is an indefinable, infinite emotion. Perhaps the most powerful of feelings, it can be beautiful, painful, and at times, all-consuming and dangerous. Whether it strikes one at first sight or blooms gradually, people cannot help falling in love . . . and then writing about it.

Love letters have been written for centuries. They were written when people sat down with quill in hand and parchment on their table, and they are written now as people type away on their cellphones and computers. Though in the contemporary times, writing personal letters is becoming a thing of the past as the world gets digitized—putting pen to paper takes longer as compared to texting or emailing; the delivery of letters takes days, sometimes even weeks.

Yet love letters are graceful in a way that texts will never be; the very image of the writer sitting with pen in hand, brooding and pining for their lover while composing heartfelt lines, evokes elegance. Though love is an emotion that often leaves people tongue-tied, countless letters have been penned to describe or confess the hold this emotion has on people.

From love that blooms in a happy marriage, to one that dare not speak its name, this edition carries letters that comprise simple confessions of love to hormone-fuelled rants, be it a king or pauper, writer or painter, common man or president. Read on to see the king of England, Henry VIII, write about the passionate love he had for his wife's lady-in-waiting, Anne Boleyn. The infamous womanizer Lord Byron flitted from one woman to another, charming and irresistible—a new day, a new woman, a new love letter. And who can forget the love-struck bard Robert Browning, who penned hundreds of letters to his beloved, Elizabeth Barrett. Their love grew intense with each letter . . . and their correspondence didn't stop even after their marriage.

The book you now hold in your hands celebrates all such, and many more delightful love letters that offer a glimpse into some unforgettable love stories.

Pliny the younger

Calpurnia

Pliny was around forty years old when he married the fourteen-year-old Calpurnia. But the difference in their age did not become an obstacle in their love. Pliny was a loving husband, and often praised his wife for her intelligence. Grief clouded their lives when Calpurnia miscarried and Pliny couldn't get the heir he wanted, but their marriage remained blissful and full of love.

c.100-113 AD

You will not believe what a longing for you possesses me. The chief cause of this is my love; and then we have not grown used to be apart. So it comes to pass that I lie awake a great part of the night, thinking of you; and that by day, when the hours return at which I was wont to visit you, my feet take me, as it is so truly said, to your chamber, but not finding you there I return, sick and sad at heart, like an excluded lover. The only time that is free from these torments is when I am being worn out at the bar, and in the suits of my friends. Judge you what must be my life when I find my repose in toil, my solace in wretchedness and anxiety. Farewell.

FROM
Henry VIII
TO
Anne Boleyn

Anne Boleyn's beauty and charm had captured the heart of the king of England. The lovesick king divorced his wife, Catherine of Aragon, and declared himself the supreme head of the Church of England so that his divorce proceedings were not obstructed.

Anne married her king, but she couldn't give him an heir. She had birthed a daughter and later suffered many miscarriages. This coupled with his suspicions that Anne had committed incest and was conspiring against him finally led him to order her execution, four months after their marriage.

The son that Henry wanted from Anne wasn't born, but ironically it was their daughter, Elizabeth, who turned out be the greatest ruler in the history of England.

May 1527

In turning over in my mind the contents of your last letters, I have put myself into great agony, not knowing how to interpret them, whether to my disadvantage, as you show in some places, or to my advantage, as I understand them in some others, beseeching you earnestly to let me know expressly your whole mind as to the love between us two.

It is absolutely necessary for me to obtain this answer, having been for above a whole year stricken with the dart of love, and not yet sure whether I shall fail of finding a place in your heart and affection, which last point has prevented me for some time past from calling you my mistress; because, if you only love me with an ordinary love, that name is not suitable for you, because it denotes a singular love, which is far from common. But if you please to do the office of a true loyal mistress and friend, and to give up yourself body and heart to me, who will be, and have been, your most loyal servant, (if your rigour does not forbid me) I promise you that not only the name shall be given you, but also that I will take you for my only mistress, casting off all others besides you out of my thoughts and affections, and serve you only. I beseech you to give an entire answer to this my rude letter, that I may know on what and how far I may depend. And if it does not please you to answer me in writing, appoint some place where I may have it by word of mouth, and I will go thither with all my heart. No more, for fear of tiring you. Written by the hand of him who would willingly remain

yours,

H. R.

❦

c.1527

My Mistress & Friend, my heart and I surrender ourselves into your hands, beseeching you to hold us commended to your favour, and that by absence your affection to us may not be lessened: for it were a great pity to increase our pain, of which absence produces enough and more than I could ever have thought could be felt, reminding us of a point in astronomy which is this: the longer the days are, the more distant is the sun, and nevertheless the hotter; so is it with our love, for by absence we are kept a distance from one another, and yet it retains its fervour, at least on my side; I hope the like on yours, assuring you that on my part the pain of absence is already too great for me; and when I think of the increase of that which I am forced to suffer, it would be almost intolerable, but for the firm hope I have of your unchangeable affection for me: and to remind you of this sometimes, and seeing that I cannot be personally present with you, I now send you the nearest thing I can to that, namely, my picture set in a bracelet, with the whole of the device, which you already know, wishing myself in their place, if it should please you.

This is from the hand of your loyal servant and friend,

H.R.

16 June 1528

There came to me suddenly in the night the most afflicting news that could have arrived. The first, to hear of the sickness of my mistress, whom I esteem more than all the world, and whose health I desire as I do my own, so that I would gladly bear half your illness to make you well. The second, from the fear that I have of being still longer harassed by my enemy. Absence, much longer, who has hitherto given me all possible uneasiness, and as far as I can judge is determined to spite me more because I pray God to rid me of this troublesome tormentor. The third, because the physician in whom I have most confidence, is absent at the very time when he might do me the greatest pleasure; for I should hope, by him and his means, to obtain one of my chief joys on earth—that is the care of my mistress—yet for want of him I send you my second, and hope that he will soon make you well. I shall then love him more than ever. I beseech you to be guided by his advice in your illness. In so doing I hope soon to see you again, which will be to me a greater comfort than all the precious jewels in the world.

Written by that secretary, who is, and for ever will be, your loyal and most assui'ed Servant,

H. (A B) R.

Michelangelo

Tommaso Cavalieri

One afternoon, the sculptor Pier Antonio Cecchini paid Michelangelo a visit, but he didn't come alone. Together with him he brought someone who would dominate Michelangelo's thoughts till the day he died—Tommaso Cavalieri.

The painter was instantly besotted with the handsome man, almost three decades younger than him. Though his love was unrequited, Michelangelo was plagued by an all-consuming passion, which tormented him but also inspired many of his paintings.

July 28, 1533

My dear Lord,

Had I not believed that I had made you certain of the very great, nay, measureless love I bear you, it would not have seemed strange to me nor have roused astonishment to observe the great uneasiness you show in your last letter, lest, through my not having written, I should have forgotten you. Still it is nothing new or marvellous when so many other things go counter, that this also should be topsy-turvy. For what your lordship says to me, I could say to yourself: nevertheless, you do this perhaps to try me, or to light a new and stronger flame, if that indeed were possible: but be it as it will: I know well that, at this hour, I could as easily forget your name as the food by which I live; nay, it were easier to forget the food, which only nourishes my body miserably, than your name, which nourishes both body and soul, filling the one and the other with such sweetness that neither weariness nor fear of death is felt by me while memory preserves you to my mind. Think, if the eyes could also enjoy their portion, in what condition I should find myself.

Catherine of Aragon

Henry VIII

Catherine of Aragon was a Spanish princess. She was the first wife of Henry VIII and Queen of England in 1509. They lived happily in the first few years of their marriage. Henry was eagerly waiting for his heir to be born, but all the sons that Catherine birthed, died. Their only surviving child was their daughter, Mary I.

Realizing that there was no promise of a male heir from Catherine, Henry VIII started to go after Catherine's lady-in-waiting, Anne Boleyn. He requested the pope to annul his marriage, claiming that it was cursed. He should have never married his brother's widow. But the Pope refused, afraid of angering Catherine's nephew, the Holy Roman Emperor, Charles V.

Henry VIII then passed the Act of Supremacy and declared himself the head of the Church of England and appointed Thomas Cranmer as Archbishop of Canterbury, who annulled Henry's marriage to Catherine.

7 January 1536

My most dear lord, king and husband,

The hour of my death now drawing on, the tender love I owe you forceth me, my case being such, to commend myself to you, and to put you in remembrance with a few words of the health and safeguard of your soul which you ought to prefer before all worldly matters, and before the care and pampering of your body, for the which you have cast me into many calamities and yourself into many troubles. For my part, I pardon you everything, and I wish to devoutly pray God that He will pardon you also. For the rest, I commend unto you our daughter Mary, beseeching you to be a good father unto her, as I have heretofore desired. I entreat you also, on behalf of my maids, to give them marriage portions, which is not much, they being but three. For all my other servants I solicit the wages due them, and a year more, lest they be unprovided for. Lastly, I make this vow, that mine eyes desire you above all things.

Sir Christopher Hatton
Queen Elizabeth

Elizabeth first laid eyes on the handsome Christopher Hatton in a play. His exquisite dancing and graceful form won the queen's respect and admiration. In 1571, he was appointed a Member of the Parliament.

There is no proof that they were lovers but the affection and yearning is apparent in Hatton's letters. Rumours about their alleged affair abounded in Elizabeth's court. Some even believed that Hatton had never married because he considered it a betrayal to his beloved queen.

1573

If I could express my feelings of your gracious letters, I should utter unto you matter of strange effect. In reading of them, with my tears I blot them; in thinking of them I feel so great comfort that I find cause, as God knoweth, to thank you on my knees. Death had been much more to my advantage than to win health and life by so loathsome a pilgrimage. The time of two days hath drawn me further from you than ten, when I return, can lead me towards you. Madam, I find the greatest lack that ever poor wretch sustained. No death, no, not hell, no fear of death, shall ever win of me my consent so far to wrong myself again as to be absent from you one day. God grant my return. I will perform this vow. I lack that I live by. The more I find this lack, the further I go from you. Shame whippeth me forward. Shame take them that counselled me to it. The life (as you well remember) is too long that loathsomely lasteth. A true saying, Madam; believe him that hath proved it. The great wisdom I find in your letters with your country counsels are very notable; but the last word is worth the Bible. Truth, truth, truth! Ever may it dwell with you. I will ever deserve it. My spirit and soul, I feel, agreeth with my body and life, that to serve you is a heaven, but to lack you is more than a hell's torment unto them. My heart is full of woe. Pardon, for God's sake, my tedious writing. It doth much diminish (for the time) my great griefs. I will wash away the faults of these letters with the drops from your poor 'lids' and so enclose them. Would God I were with you but for one hour! My wits are overwrought with thoughts. I find myself amazed. Bear with me, my most sweet, dear lady. Passion overcometh me; I can write no more. Love me, for I love you. God, I beseech thee witness the same in the behalf of thy poor servant. Live forever! Shall I utter this familiar term (farewell?) yea, ten thousand thou sand farewells. He speaketh it that most dearly loveth you. I hold you too long. Once again I crave pardon, and so bid your own poor 'Lids' farewell.

Your bondsman everlastingly tied,

Ch. Hatton.

Robert Devereux

Queen Elizabeth

Elizabeth's alleged affair to the second earl of Essex, Robert Devereaux, was a love that led to his execution. Devereaux was Robert Dudley's stepson. Allegedly, Elizabeth's affection for Dudley was transferred to his stepson after Dudley's death.

Devereaux was fiercely ambitious and temperamental. In 1599, the Queen sent him with an army to crush the rebellion brewing in Ireland. Rather than doing what he was instructed, he secretly established a truce with the Earl of Tyrone, thinking that he would explain his decision to the queen later. Elizabeth was furious and had him imprisoned. Though he was released a year later, his earlier position of power was not renewed for him.

Devastated, he banded together with some other nobles and formulated a plan to capture the queen, declaring James VI as her rightful successor. The rebellion collapsed and Devereaux was executed for conspiring against the queen.

c.1594

Madam,

The delights of this place cannot make me unmindful of one in whose sweet company I have joyed as much as the happiest man doth in his highest contentment; and if my horse could run as fast as my thoughts do fly, I would as often make mine eyes rich in beholding the treasure of my love, as my desires do triumph when I seem to myself in a strong imagination to conquer your resisting will. Noble and dear lady, tho' I be absent, let me in your favour be second unto none; and when I am at home, if I have no right to dwell chief in so excellent a place, yet I will usurp upon all the world. And so making myself as humble to do you service, as in my love I am ambitious I wish your Majesty all your happy desires. Croydon, this Tuesday, going to be mad and make my horse tame. Of all the men the most devoted to your service.

R. ESSEX.

Walter Raleigh
Elizabeth Raleigh

Elizabeth Throckmorton was Queen Elizabeth's royal attendant, and could not get married without her queen's permission. But she secretly married Walter Raleigh, the queen's favourite in her court at the time.

The queen was furious when she heard about their marriage; she put them behind bars in The Tower of London. Raleigh was back in the parliament by 1593 but had lost the queen's trust by then.

1618

You shall now receive, my dear wife, my last words, in these my last lines, my love I send you, that you may keep it when I am dead, and my counsel that you may remember it when I am no more. I would not by my will present you with sorrows, dear Bess. Let them go into the grave with me, and be buried in the dust. And seeing it is not the will of God that I shall see you any more in this life, bear it patiently, and with a heart like thyself.

First, I send you all the thanks which my heart can conceive or my words can express for your many travails and care taken for me, which, though they have not taken effect, as you wished, yet my debt to you is not the less; but pay it I never shall in this world.

Secondly, I beseech you, for the love you bare me living, do not hide yourself many days after my death, but by your travails seek to help your miserable fortunes, and the right of your poor child. Thy mournings cannot avail me, I am but dust.

Thirdly, you shall understand that my land was conveyed bona-fide to my child. The writings were drawn at Midsummer twelve months, my honest Cousin Brett can testify so much, and Dalberrie, too, can remember somewhat therein. And I trust my blood will quench their malice that have thus cruelly murthered me; and that they will not seek also to kill thee and thine with extreme poverty.

To what friend to direct thee, I know not, for all mine have left me in the true time of trial; and I plainly perceive that my death was determined from the first day.

Most sorry I am, God knows, that being thus surprised with death, I can leave you in no better state. God is my witness, I meant you all my office of wines, or all that I could have purchased by selling it, half my stuff, and all my jewels; but some on't for the boy. But God hath prevented all my resolutions, and even that great God that ruleth all in all. But if you can live free from want, care for no more; the rest is but vanity.

Love God, and begin betimes, to repose yourself on Him, and therein shall you find true and lasting riches, and endless comfort. For the rest, when you have travailled and wearied all your thoughts over all sorts of worldly cogitations, you shall but sit down by sorrow in the end.

Teach your son also to love and fear God whilst he is yet young, that the fear of God may grow up with him; and the same God will be a husband to you, and a father to him, husband and a father which cannot be taken from you.

Baylie oweth me £200 and Adrian Gilbert £600. In Jersey, I have also much money owing me, besides the arrears of the Wines will pay my debts. And howsoever you do, for my soul's sake, pay all poor men.

When I am gone, no doubt you shall be sought by many; for the world thinks that I was very rich. But take heed of the pretences of men, and their affections; for they last not but in honest, and worthy men; and no greater misery can befall you in this life than to become a prey, and afterwards to be despised. I speak not this, God knows, to dissuade you from marriage, for it will be best for you, both in respect of the world and of God.

As for me, I am no more yours, nor you mine. Death hath cut us asunder; and God hath divided me from the world, and you from me.

Remember your poor child, for his father's sake, who chose you, and loved you in his happiest times.

Get those letters (if it be possible) which I wrote to the Lords, wherein I sued for my life. God is my witness, it was for you and yours I desired life. But it is true that I disdain myself for begging it; for know it, dear wife, that your son is the son of a true man, and one, who in his own respect, despiseth death and all his misshapen and ugly shapes.

I cannot write much. God knows how hardly I steal this time, while others sleep; and it is also high time that I should separate my thoughts from the world.

Beg my dead body, which living was denied thee; and either lay it at Shirbourne (if the land continue) or in Exeter Church by my Father and Mother.

I can say no more, time and death call me away.

The everlasting, powerful, infinite and omnipotent God, that Almighty God who is goodness itself, the true life, and true light, keep thee, and thine; have mercy on me, and teach me to forgive my persecutors and accusers, and send us to meet in His glorious kingdom.

My dear wife, farewell. Bless my poor boy, pray for me, and let my good God, hold you both in His arms.

Written with the dying hand of sometime thy Husband but now (alas) overthrown. Yours that was, but now not my own.

Raleigh

Thomas Otway

Mrs. Barry

The playwright Thomas Otway's passionate love for the woman who acted in his plays was returned with an equal amount of disdain. He relentlessly pursued her, knowing that she was the Earl of Rochester's mistress.

Seeing his love in the arms of someone else was agony, yet he pined for her.

c.1678-88

My Tyrant,—I endure too much torment to be silent, and have endured it too long not to make the severest complaint. I love you; I dote on you; my love makes me mad when I am near you, and despair when I am from you. Sure, of all miseries love is to me the most intolerable; it haunts me in my sleep, perplexes me when waking; every melancholy thought makes my fears more powerful, and every delightful one makes my wishes more unruly. In all other uneasy chances of a man's life, there's an immediate re course to some kind of succour or another: in want, we apply to our friends; in sickness, to physicians; but love—the sum, the total of all misfortunes—must be endured in silence; no friend so dear to trust with such a secret, nor remedy in art so powerful to remove its anguish. Since the first day I saw you I have hardly enjoyed one day of perfect quiet. I loved you early; and no sooner had I beheld that bewitching face of yours than I felt in my heart the very foundation of all my peace give way; but when you became another's, I must confess that I did then rebel,—had foolish pride enough to promise myself that I would recover my liberty, in spite of my enslaved nature; I swore against myself I would not love you; I affected a resentment, stifled my spirit, and would not let it bend so much as once to upbraid you. Each day it was my chance to see or be near you; with stubborn sufferance I resolved to bear and brave your power,—nay, did it too, often successfully. Generally, with wine or conversation I diverted or appeased the demon that possessed me; but when at night, returning to my unhappy self, to give my heart an account why I had done it so unnatural a violence, it was then I always paid a treble interest for the short moments of ease which I had borrowed; then every treacherous thought rose up, and opened those sluices of tears that were to flow till morning. This has been for some years my best condition; nay, time itself, that decays all things else, has but increased and added to my longings. I tell you, and charge you to believe it as you are generous (which sure you must be, for everything except your neglect of me persuades me you are so), even at this time, though other arms have held you, that I love you with that tenderness of spirit, that purity of truth, that sincerity of heart, that I could sacrifice the nearest friends or interests I have on earth barely to please you. If I had all the world, it should be yours; for with it I could but be miserable, were you not mine.

I appeal to yourself for justice, if through the whole actions of my life I have done any one thing that might not let you see how absolute your authority was over me. Your commands have been sacred to me; your smiles have transported, your frowns awed me. In short, you will quickly become to me the greatest blessing or the greatest curse that ever man was doomed to. I cannot so much as look on you without confusion. You only can, with the healing cordial love, assuage and calm my torments.

Pity the man, then, that would be proud to die for you, and cannot live without you, and allow him thus far to boast that you never were beloved by a creature that had a nobler or juster pretence to your heart than the

Unfortunate

Otway.

ఎ◌⊙◌ఎ

c.1678-1688

Could I see you without passion, or be absent from you without pain, I need not beg your pardon for thus renewing my vows, that I love you more than health, or any happiness here or hereafter. Everything you do is a new charm to me; and though I have languished for seven long years, jealously despairing, yet every minute I see you I still discover something more bewitching.

Consider how I love you. What would I not renounce or undertake for you? I must have you mine, or I am miserable; and nothing but knowing which shall be the happy hour can make the rest of my life that is to come tolerable. Give me a word or two of comfort, or resolve never to look on me more; for I cannot bear a kind look, and then a cruel repulse. This minute my heart aches for you; and if I cannot have a right in yours, I wish it would ache till I could complain to you no longer. Remember poor

Otway.

William Congreve

Arabella Hunt

The following letter was written by the distinguished playwright William Congreve to his paramour, Arabella Hunt.

Arabella was married at the time. But her marriage was over the moment she found out that the man she had married was actually a crossdressing woman.

c.17th century

To Mrs. Arabella Hunt

Dear Madam

Not believe that I love you? You cannot pretend to be so incredulous. If you do not believe my tongue, consult my eyes, consult your own. You will find by yours that they have charms; by mine that I have a heart which feel them. Recall to mind what happened last night. That at least was a lover's kiss. Its eagerness, its fierceness, its warmth, expressed the God its parent. But oh! Its sweetness, and its melting softness expressed him more. With trembling in my limbs, and fevers in my soul, I ravish'd it. Convulsions, panting, murmurings shew'd the mighty disorder within me: the mighty disorder increased by it. For those dear lips shot through my heart, and thro' my bleeding vitals, delicious poison, and an avoidless but yet a charming ruin.

What cannot a day produce? The night before I thought myself a happy man, in want of nothing, and in fairest expectation of fortune; approved of by men of wit, and applauded by others. Please, nay charmed with my friends, my then dearest friends, sensible of every delicate pleasure, and in their turns possessing all.

But love, almighty love, seems in a moment to have removed me to a prodigious distence from every object but you alone. In the midst of crowds I remain in solitude. Nothing but you can lay hold of my mind, and that can lay hold of nothing but you. I appear transported to some foreign desert with you (oh, that I were really thus tranported!), where, abundantly supplied with everything, in thee, i might live out an age of uninterrupted ecstasy.

Then scene of the world's great stage seems suddenly and sadly chang'd. Unlovely objects are all around me, excepting thee; the charms of all the world appear to be translated to thee. Thus in this sad, but oh, too pleased state my soul can fix upon nothing but thee; thee it contemplates, admires, adores, nay depends on, trusts on you alone.

If you and hope forsake it, despair and endless misery attend it.

George Farquhar

Anne Oldfield

Anne had taken up apprenticeship as a seamstress, but drama was where her interests lay. One day, she paid a visit to a tavern owned by one of her family members. It was then decided that she would entertain the patrons by reciting some lines from The Scornful Lady, *and in the audience sat the dramatist George Farquhar. The beautiful and talented girl captured his heart there and then.*

c.1700

Madam,—If I ha'n't begun thrice to write and as often thrown away my pen, may I never take it up again. My head and my heart have been at cuffs about you these two long hours. Says my head, "You're a coxcomb for troubling your noddle about a lady whose beauty is as much above your pretensions as your merit is below her love."

Then answers my heart, "Good Mr. Head, you're a blockhead; I know Mr. Farquhar's merit better than you. As for your part, I know you to be as whimsical as the Devil, and changing with every new notion that offers; but for my share, I am fixed, and can stick to my opinion of a lady's merit forever; and if the fair She can secure an interest in me, Monsieur Head, you may go whistle."

"Come, come," answered my head, "you, Mr. Heart, are always leading this gentleman into some inconvenience or other. Was it not you that first enticed him to talk to this lady? Your confounded warmth made him like this lady, and your busy impertinence has made him write to her; your leaping and skipping disturbs his sleep by night and his good-humour by day. In short, sir, I will hear no more of it. I am head, and I will be obeyed."

"You lie," replied my heart, very angry. "I am head in matters of love; and if you don't give your consent, you shall be forced, for I am sure that in this case all the members will be on my side. What say you, gentlemen Hands?"

"Oh," say the hands, "we would not forego the

pleasure of pressing a delicious, white, soft hand for the world."

"Well, what say you, Mr. Tongue?"

"Zounds!" says the linguist, "there is more ecstasy in speaking three soft words of Mr. Heart's suggesting than whole orations of Signior Head's. So I am for the lady, and here's honest neighbour Lips will stick to it."

"By the sweet power of kisses, that we will," replied the lips; and thus all the worthy members standing up for the Heart, they laid violent hands (nemine contradicente) upon poor Head, and knocked out his brains. So now, Madam, behold me as perfect a lover as any in Christendom, my heart purely dictating every word I say; the little rebel throws itself into your power, and if you don't support it in the cause it has taken up for your sake, think what will be the condition of

the headless and heartless
Farquhar.

Laurence Sterne

Elizabeth Lumley

Laurence and Elizabeth got married in 1741. Neither of them were happy in the marriage and it is conjectured that Sterne consistently cheated on his wife.

The following letter was written by Sterne before their marriage.

c.18th century

You bid rue tell you, my dear L., how I bore your departure for S, and whether the valley where D'Estella stands retains still its looks,—or if I think the roses or jessamines smell as sweet as when you left it. Alas! everything has lost its relish and look! The hour you left D'Estella, I took to my bed; I was worn out by fevers of all kinds, but most by that fever of the heart with which thou knowest well I have been wasting these two years, and shall continue wasting till you quit S. The good Miss S, from the fore bodings of the best of hearts, thinking I was ill, insisted upon my going to her. What can be the cause, my dear L., that I never have been able to see the face of this mutual friend but I feel my self rent to pieces? She made me stay an hour with her; and in that short space I burst into tears a dozen different times, and in such affectionate gusts of passion that she was constrained to leave the room, and sympathize in her dressing room. "I have been weeping for you both," said she, in a tone of the sweetest pity; "for poor L.'s heart,—I have long known it; her anguish is as sharp as yours, her heart as tender, her constancy as great, her virtue as heroic. Heaven brought you not together to be tormented." I could only answer her with a kind look and a heavy sigh, and returned home to your lodgings (which I have hired till your return) to resign myself to misery. Fanny had prepared me a sup per,—she is all attention to me,—but I sat over it with tears: a bitter sauce, my L., but I could eat it with no other; for the moment she began to spread my little table, my heart fainted within me. One solitary plate, one knife, one fork, one glass! I gave a thousand pensive, penetrating looks at the chair thou hast so often graced in those quiet and sentimental repasts, then laid down my knife and fork, and took out my handkerchief and clapped it across my face, and wept like a child. I do so this very moment, my L.; for, as I take up my pen, my poor pulse quickens, my pale face glows, and the tears are trickling down upon the paper as I trace the word L. O thou! blessed in thyself and in thy virtues,—blessed to all that know thee,—to me most so, because more do I know of thee than all thy sex. This is the philter, my L., by which thou hast charmed me, and by which thou wilt hold me thine, whilst virtue and faith hold this world together. This, my friend, is the plain and simple magic by which I told Miss I have won a place in that heart of thine, on which I depend so satisfied that time, or distance, or change of everything which might alarm the hearts of little men, create no uneasy suspense in mine. Wast thou to stay in S—— these seven years, thy friend, though he would grieve, scorns to doubt, or be doubted; 'tis the only exception where security is not the parent of danger.

I told you poor Fanny was all attention to me since your departure,—contrives every day bringing in the name of L. She told me last night (upon giving me some hartshorn) she had observed my illness began the very day of your departure for S;

43

that I had never held up my head, had seldom or scarce ever smiled, had fled from all society,—that she verity believed I was broken hearted, for she had never entered the room, or passed by the door, but she heard me sigh heavily,—that I neither eat, nor slept, nor took pleasure in anything as before. Judge, then, my L., can the valley look so well, or the roses and jessamine smell so sweet, as heretofore? Ah me!—but adieu!—the vesper-bell calls me from thee to my God!

L. Sterne.

Richard Steele

Mary Scurlock

Richard Steele was at his wife's funeral when he met Mary Scurlock. They met in 1706 and got married the following year.

During their courtship and marriage, he wrote close to four hundred letters to her.

Aug. 14, 1707

Madam,

I came to your house this night to wait on you; but you have commanded me to expect the happiness of seeing you at another time of more leisure. I am now under your own roof while I write; and that imaginary satisfaction of being so near you, though not in your presence, has in it something that touches me with so tender ideas, that it is impossible for me to describe their force. All great passion makes us dumb; and the highest happiness, as well as highest grief, seizes us too violently to be expressed by our words.

You are so good as to let me know I shall have the honour of seeing you when I next come here. I will live upon that expectation, and meditate on your perfections till that happy hour. The vainest woman upon earth never saw in her glass half the attractions which I view in you. Your air, your shape, your every glance, motion, and gesture, have such peculiar graces, that you possess my whole soul, and I know no life but in the hopes of your approbation: I know not what to say, but that I love you with the sincerest passion that ever entered the heart of man. I will make it the business of my life to find out means of convincing you that I prefer you to all that's pleasing upon earth. I am, Madam, your most obedient, most faithful humble servant.

Sept. 13, 1708.

Dear Prue,

I write to you in obedience to what you ordered me, but there are not words to express the tenderness I have for you. Love is too harsh a word for it; but if you knew how my heart aches when you speak an unkind word to me, and springs with joy when you smile upon me, I am sure you would place your glory rather in preserving my happiness, like a good wife, than tormenting me like a peevish beauty. Good Prue, write me word you shall be overjoyed at my return to you, and pity the awkward figure I make when I pretend to resist you, by complying always with the reasonable demands of

Your enamoured husband,
Rich. Steele.

Esther Vanhomrigh

Jonathan Swift (edited)

Jonathan fell in love with Esther Vanhomrigh in 1707. Despite the vast age gap between them, their intense relationship lasted for seventeen years.

Things went sideways when Swift fell in love with another woman, Esther Johnson, whom he called 'Stella'. It is believed that Esther had found out about the affair and asked Swift to end things. Swift refused, thus ending his relationship.

June, London, 1713.

Sir,

Mr. Lewis assures me that you are now well, but will not tell me what authority he has for it. I hope he is rightly informed; though 'tis not my usual custom, when a thing of consequence is in doubt, to fix on what I earnestly wish. But I have already suffered so much by knowing that you were ill, and fearing you were worse then, I hope, you have been, that I will strive to change that thought, if possible, that I may have a little ease; and more, that I may not write you a splenetic letter.

Pray why would not you make Parvisol write me word how you did, when I begged it so much? And if you were able yourself, how could you be so cruel, to defer telling me the thing of the world I wished most to know? If you think I write too often, your only way is to tell me so, or at least to write to me again, that I may know you don't quite forget me; for I very much fear that I never employ a thought of yours now, except when you are reading my letters, which makes me ply you with them: (Mr. Lewis complains of you too.) If you are very happy it is ill-natured of you not to tell me so, except 'tis what is inconsistent with mine. But why don't you talk to me? That, you know, will please me. I have often heard you say that you would willingly suffer a little uneasiness, provided it gave another a vast deal of pleasure. Please remember this maxim, because it makes for me. This is now the fourth letter I have wrote to you. They could not miscarry, for they were all under Mr. Lewis's cover; nor could you avoid opening them, for the same reason . . .

Voltaire

Olympe Dunover

Voltaire's father was irritated by his son's choice of career—writing. Wishing to make his son see sense, he got him the job of a secretary to the French ambassador in Holland . . . and that was where he fell in love with Olympe Dunover. Unfortunately, both their parents disapproved of the match. Voltaire's father even thought of using a 'lettre de cachet' to stop them from being with each other. A lettre de cachet could be used by the crown to imprison someone without trial.

All this was too much for Dunover and she withdrew from the relationship, leaving Voltaire heartbroken.

The Hague 1713

I am a prisoner here in the name of the King; they can take my life, but not the love that I feel for you.

Yes, my adorable mistress, tonight I shall see you, if I had to put my head on the block to do it.

For heaven's sake, do not speak to me in such disastrous terms as you write; you must live and be cautious; beware of Madame your mother as of your worst enemy.

What do I say?

Beware of everybody; trust no one; keep yourself in readiness, as soon as the moon is visible; I shall leave the hotel incognito, take a carriage or a chaise, we shall drive like the wind to Sheveningen; I shall take paper and ink with me; we shall write our letters.

If you love me, reassure yourself; and call all your strength and presence of mind to your aid; do not let your mother notice anything, try to have your pictures, and be assured that the menace of the greatest tortures will not prevent me to serve you.

No, nothing has the power to part me from you; our love is based upon virtue, and will last as long as our lives.

Adieu, there is nothing that I will not brave for your sake; you deserve much more than that.

Adieu, my dear heart!

Arout

Alexander Pope

Teresa Blount

Alexander Pope was a man gifted with wit and intellect, but not in appearance. All he could induce in his female contemporaries was friendship, and in some cases, pity. The Blount sisters were no different. Friends with Alexander Pope since they were children, Pope had made his love for them explicit in his letters. He voiced that he loved both Martha and Teresa equally, though Teresa proclaimed that he loved Martha more.

Bath, 1714

You are to understand, Madam, that my passion for your fair self and sister has been divided with the most wonderful regularity in the world. Even from my infancy I have been in love with one after the other of you, week by week, and my journey to Bath fell out in the three hundred and seventy-sixth week of the reign of my sovereign Lady Sylvia. At the present writing hereof it is the three hundred and eighty-ninth week of the reign of your most serene majesty, in whose service I was listed some weeks before I beheld your sister. This information will account for my writing to either of you hereafter, as either shall happen to be queen-regent at that time.

Pray tell your sister all the good qualities and virtuous inclinations she has, never gave me so much pleasure in her conversation as that one vice of her obstinacy will give me mortification this month. Radcliff commands her to the Bath, and she refuses. Indeed, if I were in Berkshire, I should honour her for this obstinacy, and magnify her no less for disobedience than we do the Barcelonians. But people change with the change of places (as we see of late), and virtues become vices when they cease to be for one's interest, with me, as with others. Yet let me tell her she will never look so finely while she is upon earth as she would here in the water. It is not here as in most other instances; for those ladies that would please extremely, must go out of their own element. She does not make half so good a figure on horseback as Christina, Queen of Sweden;

but were she once seen in the Bath, no man would part with her for the best mermaid in Christendom. You know I have seen you often; I perfectly know how you look in black and white, I have experienced the utmost you can do in colours; but all your movements, all your graceful steps, deserve not half the glory you might here attain of a moving and easy behaviour in buckram—something between swimming and walking, free enough and more modestly half-naked than you can appear any where else. You have conquered enough already by land; show your ambition and vanquish also by water. I could tell you a delightful story of Dr. P, but want room to display it in all its shining circumstances. He had heard it was an excellent cure for love to kiss the aunt of the person be loved, who is generally of years and experience enough to damp the fiercest flame; he tried this course in his passion, and kissed Mrs. E at Mr. D's, but he says it will not do, and that he loves you as much as ever.

Your, &c.

Alexander Pope

Martha Blount

1714

Most Divine!—

It is some proof of my sincerity towards you, that I write when I am prepared by drinking to speak truth; and sure a letter after twelve at night must abound with that noble ingredient. That heart must have abundance of flames, which is at once warmed by wine and you: wine awakens and refreshes the lurking passions of the mind, as does the colours diat are sunk in a picture, and brings them out in all their natural glowings. My good qualities have been so frozen and locked up in a dull constitution at all my former sober hours, that it is very astonishing to me, now I am drunk, to find so much virtue in me.

In these overflowings of my heart I pay you my thanks for those two obliging letters you favoured me with of the 18th and 24th instant. That which begins with "My charming Mr. Pope!" was a delight to me beyond all expression: you have at last entirely gained the conquest over your fair sister.

It is true you are not handsome, for you are a woman, and think you are not: but this good-humour and tenderness for me has a charm that cannot be resisted. That face must needs be irresistible, which was adorned with smiles even when it could not see the coronation. I do suppose you will not show this epistle out of vanity, as I doubt not your sister does all I write to her. Indeed, to correspond with Mr. Pope, may make any one proud who lives under a dejection of heart in the country.

Every one values Mr. Pope, but every one for a different reason: one for his adherence to the Catholic faith; another for his neglect of Popish superstition; one for his grave behaviour, another for his whimsicalness; Mr. Titcomb, for his pretty atheistical jests; Mr. Caryll, for his moral and Christian sentences; Mrs. Teresa, for his reflections on Mrs. Patty; and Mrs. Patty, for his reflections on Mrs. Teresa.

It was but the other day I heard of Mrs. Fermor's being actually and directly married. I wonder how the couple at —— look, stare, and simper, since that grand secret came out, which they so well concealed before. They concealed it as well as the barber does his utensils, when he goes to trim upon a Sunday, and his towels hang out all the way. You know your Doctor is gone the way of all his patients, and was hard put to it how to dispose of an estate miserably unwieldy and splendidly unuseful to him. Dr. Shadwell lately told a lady, he wondered she could be alive after him: she made answer, she wondered at it too, both because Dr. Radcliffe was dead, and because Dr. Shadwell was alive. I am Your most faithful admirer, friend, servant, any thing, &c.

I send you Gay's poem on the princess. She is very fat. God help her husband.

Alexander Pope

FROM

Jonathan Swift

TO

Esther Vanhomrigh

c.1714

Monday Morning

I will see you in a day or two, and believe me, it goes to my soul not to see you oftener. I will give you the best advice, countenance and assistance I can. I would have been with you sooner if a thousand impediments had not prevented me. I did not imagine you had been under difficulties: I am sure my whole fortune should go to remove them. I cannot see you, I fear, today, having affairs of my place to do; but pray think it not want of friendship or tenderness, which I will always continue to the utmost.

Abigail Smith

John Adams

Abigail Smith was fifteen years old when she met John Adams in 1759.

Adams' father had given his blessings but Abigail's mother did not want her daughter marrying a mere country lawyer. She gave in eventually and the couple got married in 1764.

Braintree March 31, 1776

I wish you would ever write me a Letter half as long as I write you; and tell me if you may where your Fleet are gone? What sort of Defence Virginia can make against our common Enemy? Whether it is so situated as to make an able Defence? Are not the Gentery Lords and the common people vassals, are they not like the uncivilized Natives Brittain represents us to be? I hope their Riffel Men who have shewen themselves very savage and even Blood thirsty; are not a specimen of the Generality of the people.

I am willing to allow the Colony great merrit for having produced a Washington but they have been shamefully duped by a Dunmore.

I have sometimes been ready to think that the passion for Liberty cannot be Eaquelly Strong in the Breasts of those who have been accustomed to deprive their fellow Creatures of theirs. Of this I am certain that it is not founded upon that generous and christian principal of doing to others as we would that others should do unto us.

Do not you want to see Boston; I am fearfull of the small pox, or I should have been in before this time. I got Mr. Crane to go to our House and see what state it was in. I find it has been occupied by one of the Doctors of a Regiment, very dirty, but no other damage has been done to it. The few things which were left in it are all gone. Cranch has the key which he never deliverd up. I have wrote to him for it and am determined to get it cleand as soon as possible and shut it up. I look upon it a new acquisition of property, a property which one month ago I did not value at a single Shilling, and could with pleasure have seen it in flames.

The Town in General is left in a better state than we expected, more oweing to a percipitate flight than any Regard to the inhabitants, tho some individuals discoverd a sense of honour and justice and have left the rent of the Houses in which they were, for the owners and the furniture unhurt, or if damaged suffcient to make it good.

Others have committed abominable Ravages. The Mansion House of your President is safe and the furniture unhurt whilst both the House and Furniture of the Solisiter General have fallen a prey to their own merciless party. Surely the very Fiends feel a Reverential awe for Virtue and patriotism, whilst they Detest the paricide and traitor.

I feel very differently at the approach of spring to what I did a month ago. We knew not then whether we could plant or sow with safety, whether when we had toild we could reap the fruits of our own industery, whether we could rest in our own Cottages, or whether we should not be driven from the sea coasts to seek shelter in the wilderness, but now we feel as if we might sit under our own vine and eat the good of the land.

I feel a gaieti de Coar to which before I was a stranger. I think the Sun looks brighter, the Birds sing more melodiously, and Nature puts on a more chearfull countanance. We feel a temporary peace, and the poor fugitives are returning to their deserted habitations.

Tho we felicitate ourselves, we sympathize with those who are trembling least the Lot of Boston should be theirs. But they cannot be in similar circumstances unless pusilanimity and cowardise should take possession of them. They have time and warning given them to see the Evil and shun it. I long to hear that you have declared an indepeadency—and by the way in the new Code of Laws which I suppose it will be necessary for you to make I desire you would Remember the Ladies, and be more generous and favourable to them than your ancestors. Do not put such unlimited power into the hands of the Husbands. Remember all Men would be tyrants if they could. If perticuliar care and attention is not paid to the Laidies we are determined to foment a Rebelion, and will not hold ourselves bound by any Laws in which we have no voice, or Representation.

That your Sex are Naturally Tyrannical is a Truth so thoroughly established as to admit of no dispute, but such of you as wish to be happy willingly give up the harsh title of Master for the more tender and endearing one of Friend. Why then, not put it out of the power of the vicious and the Lawless to use us with cruelty and indignity with impunity. Men of Sense in all Ages abhor those customs which treat us only as the vassals of your Sex. Regard us then as Beings placed by providence under your protection and in immitation of the Supreem Being make use of that power only for our happiness.

Benjamin Franklin

Anne Brillon

In 1777, Benjamin Franklin moved to Paris and met Anne Louis Brillon de Juoy. Enamoured by her beauty, intellectuality, and musical talent, he tried to court her, but his attempts were in vain. Madame Brillon was married at the time, and insisted that she enjoyed his company, but only as a friend.

July 27, 1778

Madame Brillon,

What a difference, my dear friend, between you and me! You find innumerable faults with me, whereas I see only one fault in you (but perhaps that is the fault of my glasses). I mean this kind of avarice which leads you to seek monopoly on all my affection, and not allow me any for the agreeable ladies of your country.

Do you imagine that it is impossible for my affection (or my tenderness) to be divided without being diminished? You deceive yourself, and you forget the playful manner with which you stopped me. You renounce and totally exclude all that might be of the flesh in our affection, allowing me only some kisses, civil and honest, such as you might grant your little cousins. What am I receiving that is so special as to prevent me from giving the same to others, without taking from what belongs to you?

The sweet sounds brought forth from the pianoforte by your clever hand can be enjoyed by twenty people simultaneously without diminishing at all the pleasure you so obligingly mean for me, and I could, with as little reason, demand from your affection that no other ears but mine be allowed to be charmed by those sweet sounds.

Yours,
Benjamin

Robert Burns met Mrs. Mclehose on his second visit to Edinburgh. His passion for her was returned with equal force, but Burns was committed to Jean Armour at the time. Agnes was married, though her husband had left her and gone to live in West Indies. So the possibility of their union was slim. They exchanged love letters for some time but eventually, Burns moved to Ayrshire and married Jean.

Monday Evening, 11 o'clock,

Jan. 14, 1788.

Why have I not heard from you, Clarinda? Today I well expected it, and, before supper, when a letter to me was announced, my heart danced with rapture; but behold, 'twas some fool who had taken into his head to turn poet, and make me an offer of the first fruits of his nonsense. "It is not poetry, but prose run mad."

Did I ever repeat to you an epigram I made on a Mr. Elphinston, who has given a translation of Martial, a famous Latin poet? The poetry of Elphinston can only equal his prose notes. I was sitting in a merchant's shop of my acquaintance, waiting somebody; he put Elphinston into my hand, and asked my opinion of it; I begged leave to write it on a blank leaf, which I did, as you shall see on a new page:——

To Mr. Elphinstone

O thou whom poesy abhors!
Whom poesy has turned out of doors!
Heard'st thou yon groan? Proceed no
    further!
'Twas laurell'd Martial calling murther!

I am determined to see you, if at all possible, on Saturday evening. Next week I must sing:—

> "The night is my departing night,
> "The morn 's the day I must awa:
> "There's neither friend nor foe o' mine
> "But wishes that I were awa'!
> "What I hae done for lack o' wit I
>   never, never can reca';
> "I hope ye 're a' my friends as yet.
> "Gude night, and joy be wi' you a'!"

If I could see you sooner, I would be so much the happier; but I would not purchase the dearest gratification on earth, if it must be at your expense in worldly censure; far less, inward peace!

I shall certainly be ashamed of thus scrawling whole sheets of incoherence. The only unity (a sad word with poets and critics!) in my ideas is Clarinda. There my heart 'reigns and revels'.

> "What art thou, Love? whence are
>   those charms,
> "That thus thou bear'st an universal
>   rule?
> "For thee the soldier quits his arms,
> "The king turns slave, the wise man fool.

"In vain we chase thee from the field,
"And with vain thoughts resist the
     yoke:
"Next tide of blood, alas! we yield;
"And all those high resolves are broke!"

I like to have quotations ready for every occasion. They give one's ideas so pat, and save the trouble of finding expressions adequate to one's feelings. I think it is one of the greatest pleasures attending a poetic genius, that we can give our woes, cares, joys, loves, &c, an embodied form in verse, which, to me, is ever immediate ease. Goldsmith finely says of his muse:—

"Thou source of all my bliss and all
     my woe;
"Who found me poor at first, and
     keep'st me so."

My limb has been so well today that I have gone up and down stairs often without my staff. Tomorrow I hope to walk once again on my own legs to dinner. It is only next street. Adieu!

Sylvander.

Mozart

Constanze Weber

When Mozart started living with the Weber family, he had no idea he would end up falling for the sister of his old flame. He had stopped pining for Aloysia Weber, who had married someone else by then, and instead his eyes darted towards Constanze. He found her and her singing, incredibly beautiful. Constanze reciprocated his love and both got married in 1782, even though Mozart's father disapproved of the match.

16 April 1789

Dear little wife, I have a number of requests to make. I beg you.

(1) not to be melancholy,

(2) to take care of your health and to beware of the spring breezes,

(3) not to go out walking alone—and preferably not to go out walking at all,

(4) to feel absolutely assured of my love. Up to the present I have not written a single letter to you without placing your dear portrait before me.

(5) and lastly I beg you to send me more details in your letters. I should very much like to know whether after my departure? Whether he comes very often, as he promised me he would? Whether the Langes come sometimes? Whether progress is being made with the portrait? What sort of life you are leading? All these things are naturally of great interest to me.

(6) I beg in your conduct not only to be careful of your honour and mine, but also to consider appearances. Do not be angry with me for asking this. You ought to love me even more for thus valuing our honour.

W. A. Mozart

September 1790

Dearest little Wife of my heart!

If only I had a letter from you, everything would be all right . . .

Dearest, I have no doubt that I shall get something going here, but it won't be easy as you and some of our friends think.—It is true, I am known and respected here; but, well—No—let us just see what happens.—In any case, I do prefer to play it safe, that why I would like to conclude this deal with H . . . because I would get some money into my possession without having to pay any out; all I would have to do then is work, and I shall be only too happy to do that for my little wife.

I get all excited like a child when I think about being with you again—If people could see into my heart I should almost feel ashamed. Everything is cold to me—ice-cold.—If you were here with me, maybe I would find the courtesies people are showing me more enjoyable,—but as it is, it's all so empty—adieu—my dear—I am Forever

your Mozart who loves you
with his entire soul.

PS.—while I was writing the last page, tear after tear fell on the paper. But I must cheer up—catch—An astonishing number of kisses are flying about—The deuce!—I see a whole crowd of them. Ha! Ha! . . . I have just caught three—They are delicious . . . I kiss you millions of times.

Mary Wollstonecraft

Gilbert Imlay

Captain Gilbert Imlay, a former soldier, a successful entrepreneur, and a notorious womanizer met Mary Wollstonecraft in Paris. Mary was clearly in love with him but a man of his moral character could not be bound in matrimony.

When Mary got pregnant with his child, he reluctantly registered her as his wife in the American Embassy. In their later married life, he was consistently unfaithful. Distressed, Mary attempted to take her life, but even such an extreme decision didn't coax him to be with her. The couple separated in 1796.

Past twelve o'clock, Monday night

Paris, Aug. 1793

I obey an emotion of my heart, which made me think of wishing thee, my love, goodnight! before I go to rest, with more tenderness than I can tomorrow, when writing a hasty line or two under Colonel——'s eye. You can scarcely imagine with what pleasure I anticipate the day, when we are to begin almost to live together; and you would smile to hear how many plans of employment I have in my head, now that I am confident my heart has found peace in your bosom.—Cherish me with that dignified tenderness, which I have only found in you; and your own dear girl will try to keep under a quickness of feeling, that has sometimes given you pain.—Yes, I will be good, that I may deserve to be happy; and whilst you love me, I cannot again fall into the miserable state, which rendered life a burthen almost too heavy to be borne.

But, goodnight!—God bless you! Sterne says, that is equal to a kiss—yet I would rather give you the kiss into the bargain, glowing with gratitude to Heaven, and affection to you. I like the word affection, because it signifies something habitual;

and we are soon to meet, to try whether we have mind enough to keep our hearts warm.

I will be at the barrier a little after ten o'clock tomorrow.

Mary.

ᏹᎣᏫᎣᏫ

23 September 1794

I have been playing and laughing with the little girl so long, that I cannot take up my pen to address you without emotion. Pressing her to my bosom, she looked so like you (entre nous, your best looks, for I do not admire your commercial face), every nerve seemed to vibrate to the touch, and I began to think that there was something in the assertion of man and wife being one for you seemed to pervade my whole frame, quickening the beat of my heart, and lending me the sympathetic tears you excited.

Have I anything more to say to you? No; not for the present—the rest is all flown away; and indulging tenderness for you, I cannot now complain of some people here, who have ruffled my temper for two or three days past.

Napoleon Bonaparte

Josephine De Beauharnais

Napoleon was just an army officer when he met Josèphe Rose Tascher de la Pagerie, an aristocrat's daughter. He called her Josephine. They were introduced to each other by Paul Barras, who was Josephine's lover at the time.

Josephine fell in love with the handsome officer who was six years younger to her. They got married in a beautiful and interesting ceremony—the person conducting the ceremony wasn't qualified to do so, the bride had to lie about her age, and the groom had to give a false address and date of birth.

Despite such efforts their marriage didn't last. Napoleon started thinking of divorcing her since she couldn't give him an heir. Also, it didn't help Josephine's case when Napoleon found out that she had had an affair while he had gone to fight. They separated in 1807.

1796

Seven o'clock in the morning.

My waking thoughts are all of thee. Your portrait and the remembrance of last night's delirium have robbed my senses of repose. Sweet and incomparable Josephine, what an extraordinary influence you have over my heart. Are you vexed? do I see you sad? are you ill at ease? My soul is broken with grief, and there is no rest for your lover. But is there more for me when, delivering ourselves up to the deep feelings which master me, I breathe out upon your lips, upon your heart, a flame which burns me up—ah, it was this past night I realised that your portrait was not you. You start at noon; I shall see you in three hours. Meanwhile, *mio dolce amor*, accept a thousand kisses, but give me none, for they fire my blood.

N. B.

Chanceaux Post House,
March 14, 1796.

I wrote you at Chatillon, and sent you a power
of attorney to enable you to receive various sums
of money in course of remittance to me. Every
moment separates me further from you, my
beloved, and every moment I have less energy
to exist so far from you. You are the constant
object of my thoughts; I exhaust my imagination
in thinking of what you are doing. If I see you
unhappy, my heart is torn, and my grief grows
greater. If you are gay and lively among your friends
(male and female), I reproach you with having so
soon forgotten the sorrowful separation three days
ago; thence you must be fickle, and henceforward
stirred by no deep emotions. So you see I am not
easy to satisfy; but, my dear, I have quite different
sensations when I fear that your health may be
affected, or that you have cause to be annoyed;
then I regret the haste with which I was separated
from my darling. I feel, in fact, that your natural
kindness of heart exists no longer for me, and it is
only when I am quite sure you are not vexed that
I am satisfied. If I were asked how I slept, I feel
that before replying I should have to get a message
to tell me that you had had a good night. The

ailments, the passions of men influence me only when I imagine they may reach you, my dear. May my good genius, which has always preserved me in the midst of great dangers, surround you, enfold you, while I will face my fate unguarded. Ah! be not gay, but a trifle melancholy; and especially may your soul be free from worries, as your body from illness: you know what our good Ossian says on this subject. Write me, dear, and at full length, and accept the thousand and one kisses of your most devoted and faithful friend.

Port Maurice, April 3, 1796

I have received all your letters, but none has affected me like the last. How can you think, my charmer, of writing me in such terms? Do you believe that my position is not already painful enough without further increasing my regrets and subverting my reason. What eloquence, what feelings you portray; they are of fire, they inflame my poor heart! My unique Josephine, away from you there is no more joy—away from thee the world is a wilderness, in which I stand alone, and without experiencing the bliss of unburdening my soul. You have robbed me of more than my soul; you are the one only thought of my life. When I am weary of the worries of my profession, when I mistrust the issue, when men disgust me, when I am ready to curse my life, I put my hand on my heart where your portrait beats in unison. I look at it, and love is for me complete happiness; and everything laughs for joy, except the time during which I find myself absent from my beloved.

By what art have you learnt how to captivate all my faculties, to concentrate in yourself my spiritual existence—it is witchery, dear love, which will end only with me. To live for Josephine, that is the history of my life. I am struggling to get near you, I am dying to be by your side; fool that I am, I fail to realise how far off I am, that lands and provinces separate us. What an age it will be before you read these lines, the weak expressions of the fevered soul in which you reign. Ah, my winsome wife, I know not what fate awaits me, but if it keeps me much longer from you it will be unbearable— my strength will not last out. There was a time in which I prided myself on my strength, and, sometimes, when casting my eyes on the ills which men might do me, on the fate that destiny might have in store for me, I have gazed steadfastly on the most incredible misfortunes without a wrinkle on my brow or a vestige of surprise: but today the thought that my Josephine might be ill; and, above all, the cruel, the fatal thought that she might love me less, blights my soul, stops my blood, makes me wretched and dejected, without even leaving me the courage of fury and despair. I often used to say that men have no power over him who dies without regrets; but, today, to die without your love, to die in uncertainty of that, is the torment of hell, it is a lifelike and terrifying figure of absolute annihilation—I feel passion strangling me. My unique companion! you whom Fate has destined to walk with me the painful path of life! the day on which I no longer possess your heart will be that on which parched Nature will be for me without warmth and without vegetation. I stop, dear love! my soul is sad, my body tired, my spirit dazed, men worry me—I ought indeed to detest them; they keep me from my beloved.

I am at Port Maurice, near Oneille; tomorrow I shall be at Albenga. The two armies are in motion. We are trying to deceive each other—victory to the most skilful! I am pretty well satisfied with Beaulieu; he need be a much stronger man than his predecessor to alarm me much. I expect to give him a good drubbing. Don't be anxious; love me as thine eyes, but that is not enough; as thyself, more than thyself; as thy thoughts, thy mind, thy sight, thy all. Dear love, forgive me, I am exhausted; nature is weak for him who feels acutely, for him whom you inspire.

Kind regards to Barras, Sussi, Madame Tallien; compliments to Madame Chateau Renard; to Eugène and Hortense best love. Adieu, adieu! I lie down without thee, I shall sleep without thee; I pray thee, let me sleep. Many times I shall clasp thee in my arms, but, but—it is not thee.

April 24, 1796

To My Sweet Love.—My brother will remit you this letter. I have for him the most lively affection. I trust he will obtain yours; he merits it. Nature has endowed him with a gentle, even, and unalterably good disposition; he is made up of good qualities. I am writing Barras to help him to the Consulate of some Italian port. He wishes to live with his little wife far from the great whirlwind, and from great events. I recommend him to you. I have received your letters of (April) the fifth and tenth. You have been several days without writing me. What are you doing then? Yes, my kind, kind love,

I am not jealous, but sometimes uneasy. Come soon. I warn you, if you tarry you will find me ill; fatigue and your absence are too much for me at the same time.

Your letters make up my daily pleasure, and my happy days are not often. Junot bears to Paris twenty-two flags. You ought to return with him, do you understand? Be ready, if that is not disagreeable to you. Should he not come, woe without remedy; should he come back to me alone, grief without consolation, constant anxiety. My Beloved, he will see you, he will breathe on your temples; perhaps you will accord him the unique and priceless favour of kissing your cheek, and I, I shall be alone and very far away; but you are about to come, are you not? You will soon be beside me, on my breast, in my arms, over your mouth. Take wings, come quickly, but travel gently. The route is long, bad, fatiguing. If you should be overturned or be taken ill, if fatigue—go gently, my beloved.

I have received a letter from Hortense. She is entirely lovable. I am going to write to her. I love her much, and I will soon send her the perfumes that she wants.

N. B.

I don't know if you need money; you have never talked about your affairs. If so, you can ask my brother, who has 200 louis of mine.

Verona, November 23, 1796.

I don't love you an atom; on the contrary, I detest you. You are a good for nothing, very ungraceful, very tactless, very tatterdemalion. You never write to me; you don't care for your husband; you know the pleasure your letters give him, and you write him barely half-a-dozen lines, thrown off anyhow.

How, then, do you spend the livelong day, madam? What business of such importance robs you of the time to write to your very kind lover? What inclination stifles and alienates love, the affectionate and unvarying love which you promised me? Who may this paragon be, this new lover who engrosses all your time, is master of your days, and prevents you from concerning yourself about your husband? Josephine, be vigilant; one fine night the doors will be broken in, and I shall be before you.

Truly, my dear, I am uneasy at getting no news from you. Write me four pages immediately, and some of those charming remarks which fill my heart with the pleasures of imagination.

I hope that before long I shall clasp you in my arms, and cover you with a million kisses as burning as if under the equator.

Bonaparte.

William Godwin

Mary Wollstonecraft

William Godwin was a well-known writer when Mary fell in love with him. Their relationship began in 1796 but neither of them had any marriage plans . . . until Mary got pregnant with William's child. Even so, their marriage was a happy one. Unfortunately, Mary and William couldn't stay married for more than six months since Mary died after giving birth to their daughter.

October 4, 1796

So I must write a line to sweeten your dinner— No; to give you a little salt for your mutton, rather: though your not partaking of a morsel, Mary was bringing me up, of this dinner, as you were going out, prevented me from relishing it—

I should have liked to have dined with you today, after finishing your essay—that my eyes, and lips, I do not exactly mean my voice, might have told you that they had raised you in my esteem. What a cold word! I would say love, if you will promise not to dispute about its propriety, when I want to express an increasing affection, founded on a more intimate acquaintance with your heart and understanding.

I shall cork up all my kindness—yet the fine volatile essence may fly off in my walk—you know not how much tenderness for you may escape in a voluptuous sigh, should the air, as is often the case, give a pleasurable movement to the sensations, that have been clustering round my heart, as I read this morning—reminding myself, every now and then, that the writer loved me. Voluptuous is often expressive of a meaning I do not now intend to give, I would describe one of those moments, when the senses are exactly tuned by the ringing tenderness of the heart and according reason entices you to live in the present moment, regardless of the past or future—it is not rapture—it is sublime tranquility. I have felt it in your arms—hush! Let not the light see, I was going to say hear it—these confessions should only be uttered—you know where, when the curtains are up—and all the world shut out—

Ah me! What shall I do today, I anticipate the unpleasing task of repressing kindness—and I am overflowing with the kindest sympathy—I wish I may find you at home when I carry this letter to drop it in the box,—that I may drop a kiss with it into your heart, to be embalmed, till me meet, closer (Mary drew a line over the word 'closer' and added the following line.) Don't read the last word—I charge you!

Lord Nelson

Lady Hamilton

Lord Nelson was referred to as a man who was 'as brave as a lion and as gentle as a lamb'. His genuine love for the irresistible Lady Hamilton began when they first met each other at Naples, and only ended with Nelson's death at the battle of Trafalgar.

March 17, 1801.

My dearest friend,

I have bought your picture, for I could not bear it should be put up at auction, and if it had cost me 300 drops of blood I would have given it with pleasure. I think the picture had better be delivered to Mr. Davison packed up, and I have charged him not to mention it, or to chew it to any soul breathing. I design it always to hang in my bedchamber, and if I die it is yours. After we get into the Baltic it may be very dangerous writing, for if the vessel is taken, which is very probable, my correspondence will certainly be published, therefore I shall never sign my name in future. Heavens bless you. Send my letter and order to Mr. Christie directly.

July 29th, 1801.

My dearest Emma,

Your letter of yesterday naturally called forth all those finer feelings of the sort which none but those who regard each other as you and I do can conceive, although I am not able to write so well, and so forcibly mark my feelings as you can. Not one moment I have to myself, and my business is endless. At noon I set off for Faversham to arrange the Sea Fencibles on that part of the coast; at nine o'clock I expect to be at Deal to arrange with Admiral Lutwidge various matters; and tomorrow evening, or next day morning, to sail for the coast of France, that I may judge from my own eye, and not from those of others. Be where I may, you are always present to my thoughts—not another thing, except the duty I owe to my country, ever interferes with you.

Yours,
Nelson and Bronte.

FROM

Leigh Hunt

TO

Marianne Kent

After a few years of courtship, Leigh Hunt married Marianne Kent in 1809. But the love that had blossomed between them soon diminished. Marianne wasn't exactly a desirable partner. She had turned into an alcoholic, was a terrible mother, and had borrowed money from Hunt's friends behind his back. Even so, Hunt remained loyal to her all his life. His eldest son often commented that his Aunt Elizabeth, Marianne's sister, would have been a better match for him.

Gainsborough, Thursday, February 1806.

Dearest Girl,—My journey to Doncaster is deferred till next week, so I sit down to write you a day earlier than I intended, in order that you may have two letters instead of one this week to make up for former deficiencies. A very heavy rain last night has made the snow vanish from the fields, which look delightfully green this morning. I walked out to enjoy the lively air and the universal sunshine, and seated myself with a book on the gateway at the bottom of a little eminence covered with evergreens, a little way from Gains borough. It seemed the return of spring; a flock of sheep were grazing before me, and cast up every now and then their inquiring visages as much as to say, "What singular being is that so intent upon the mysterious thin substance he is turning over with his hand?" The crows at intervals came wheeling with long cawings above my head; the herds lowed from the surrounding farms; the windmills whirled to the breeze, flinging their huge and rapid shadows on the fields; and the river Trent sparkled in the sun from east to west. A delightful serenity diffused itself through my heart. I worshipped the magnificence and the love of the God of nature, and I thought of you. These two sensations always arise in my heart in the quiet of a rural landscape, and I have often considered it a proof of the purity and the reality of my affection for you, that it always feels most powerful in my religious moments. And this is very natural. Are you not the greatest blessing Heaven has bestowed upon me? Your image at tends my rural rambles not only in the healthful walks when, escaped from the clamour of streets and the glare of theatres, I am ready to exclaim with Cowper, 'God made the country, and man made the town.' It is present with me even in the bustle of life; it gives me a distaste to a frivolous and riotous society; it excites me to improve myself in order to deserve your affection, and it quenches the little flashes of caprice and impatience which disturb the repose of existence. If I feel my anger rising at trifles it checks me instantaneously; it seems to say to me, "Why do you disturb yourself? Marienne loves you; you deserve her love, and ought to be above these little marks of a little mind." Such is the power of love. I am naturally a man of violent passions, but your affection has taught me to subdue them.

Whenever you feel any little inquietudes or impatiences arising in your bosom, think of the happiness you bestow upon me, and real love will produce the same effect on you that it produces on me. No reasoning person ought to marry, who cannot say, "My love has made, me better, and more desirous of improvement than I was before."

. . . I do not write, I acknowledge, with the best hand in the world, but I endeavour to avoid blots or interpolations. I suppose you guess by this preamble that I am going to find fault with your letters. I would not dare, however, to find fault were I not sure that you would receive my letters cheerfulby. You have no false shame to induce you to conceal or deny your faults,—quite the contrary; you think sometimes too much of them, for I know of none which you cannot remedy. Besides, my faithful and attentive affection would induce me to ask with confidence any little sacrifice of your time and care; and as you have done so much for me in correcting the errors of my head you will not feel very unpleasant when I venture to correct the errors of your hand. Now, cannot you sit down on Sunday, my sweet girl, and write me a fair, even-minded, honest hand, unvexed with desperate blots or skulking interlineations? Mind, I do not quarrel with the contents or with the subject; what you tell me of others amuses me, and what you tell me of yourself delights me. It is merely the fashion of your lines; in short, as St. Paul saith, "It is the spirit giveth life, but the letter killeth."

Present my respects to Mrs. Hunter and tell her I have found the tune, the Scotch tune, which pleased her so much between the acts in Douglas; it belongs to a song called Tweedside, beginning, 'What beauties does Flora disclose.' I will play it to her when I return. I shall write Mrs. Hunter next week . . . It is astonishing I should ever be melancholy when I possess friends like these; and when, above all, I am able to tell my dearest Marienne how infinitely she is beloved by her

Henry.

Mary Hutchinson

William Wordsworth (edited)

Mary Hutchinson and Dorothy Wordsworth had been friends for life. They visited each other frequently, and these visits continued when Dorothy started living with her brother, William. The long, languorous hours Mary spent at the Wordsworth home sparked a fire of love between her and William. They got married in 1802.

Unlike Dorothy, Mary may not have had much influence on the poet's work, but the letters he wrote to her showcase that they passionately, and unmistakably, loved each other.

c.1810

O My William!

It is not in my power to tell thee how I have been affected by this dearest of all letters—it was so unexpected—so new a thing to see the breathing of thy inmost heart upon paper that I was quite overpowered, & now that I sit down to answer thee in the loneliness & depth of that love which unites us & which cannot be felt but by ourselves, I am so agitated & my eyes are so bedimmed that I scarcely know how to proceed—I have brought my paper, after having laid my baby upon thy sacred pillow, into my own, into THY own room—& write from Sara's little Table, retired from the window which looks upon the lasses strewing out the hay to an uncertain Sun . . .

I look upon thy letter & I marvel how thou hast managed to write it so legibly, for there is not a word in it, that I could have a doubt about. But how is it that I have not received it sooner—It was written on Sunday before last—last Sunday Morning I rec. One of Dear Dorothy's written on the Monday & another in the evening of the same day, written on the Thursday; both since that day when my good angel put it into thy thoughts to make me so happy—Dorothy has asked me more than once when she has found me this morning with thy letter in my hand what I was crying about—I told her that I was so happy—but she could not comprehend this. Indeed my love it has made me supremely blessed—it has given m e a new feeling, for it is the first letter of love that has been exclusively my own—Wonder not then that I have been so affected by it.

Dearest William! I am sorry about thy eye— that it is not well before now, & I am SORRY for what causes in me such pious & exulting gladness— that you cannot fully enjoy your absence from me— indeed William I feel, I have felt that you cannot, but it overpowers me to be told it by your own pen I was much moved by the lines written with your hand in one of D's letters where you spoke of coming home thinking you 'would be of great use' to me—indeed my love thou wouldst but I did not want thee so much then, as I do now that our uncomfortableness is passed away—if you had been here, no doubt there would have existed in me that under consciousness that I had my all in all about me—that feeling which I have never wanted since the solitary night did not separate us, except in absence; but I had not then that leisure which I ought to have & which is necessary to be actively alive to so rich a possession & to the full enjoyment of it—I do William & I shall to the end of my life consider this sacrifice as a dear offering of thy love, I feel it to be such, & I am grateful to thee for it but I trust that it will be the last of the kind that we shall need to make.

Beethoven

His Immortal Beloved

The legendary composer Beethoven penned countless letters to an unnamed recipient. The identity of this woman remains a mystery till today.

All the letters Beethoven wrote were never sent—a sad fact that indicates that maybe the lovers knew that they could never fully be with each other.

July [1801?]

On the 6th July in the morning.

My angel, my all, my very self,

Just a few words to-day, and indeed in pencil—(with thine) only till to-morrow is my room definitely engaged, what an unworthy waste of time in such matters—why this deep sorrow where necessity speaks. Can our love endure otherwise than through sacrifices, through restraint in longing. Canst thou help not being wholly mine, can I, not being wholly thine. Oh! gaze at nature in all its beauty, and calmly accept the inevitable—love demands everything, and rightly so. Thus is it for me with thee, for thee with me, only thou so easily forgettest, that I must live for myself and for thee—were we wholly united thou wouldst feel this painful fact as little as I should—my journey was terrible. I arrived here only yesterday morning at four o'clock, and as they were short of horses, the mail-coach selected another route, but what an awful road; at the last stage but one I was warned against travelling by night; they frightened me with a wood, but that only spurred me on—and I was wrong, the coach must needs break down, the road being dreadful, a swamp, a mere country road; without the postillions I had with me, I should have stuck on the way. Esterhazi, by the ordinary road, met with the same fate with eight horses as I with four—yet it gave me some pleasure, as successfully overcoming any difficulty always does. Now for a quick change from without to within; we shall probably soon see each other, besides, to-day I cannot tell thee what has been passing through my mind during the past few days concerning my life—were our hearts closely united, I should not do things of this kind. My heart is full of the many things I have to say to thee—ah!—there are moments in which I feel that speech is powerless—cheer up—remain my true, my only treasure, my all!!! as I to thee. The gods must send the rest, what for us must be and ought to be.

Thy faithful,
Ludwig.

1812

Monday evening, 6 July

Thou sufferest, thou my dearest love. I have just found out that the letters must be posted very early Mondays, Thursdays—the only days when the post goes from here to K. Thou sufferest—Ah! where I am, art thou also with me; I will arrange for myself and Thee. I will manage so that I can live with thee; and what a life!!!! But as it is!!!! without thee. Persecuted here and there by the kindness of men, which I little deserve, and as little care to deserve. Humility of man towards man—it pains me—and when I think of myself in connection with the universe, what am I and what is He who is named the Greatest; and still this again shows the divine in man. I weep when I think that probably thou wilt only get the first news from me on Saturday evening. However much thou lovest me, my love for thee is stronger, but never conceal thy thoughts from me. Good-night. As I am taking the baths I must go to bed [two words scratched through]. O God—so near! so far! Our love, is it not a true heavenly edifice, firm as heaven's vault.

Good morning, on 7 July

While still in bed, my thoughts press to thee, my Beloved One, at moments with joy, and then again with sorrow, waiting to see whether fate will take pity on us. Either I must live wholly with thee or not at all. Yes, I have resolved to wander in distant lands, until I can fly to thy arms, and feel that with thee I have a real home; with thee encircling me about, I can send my soul into the kingdom of spirits. Yes, unfortunately, it must be so. Calm thyself, and all the more since thou knowest my faithfulness towards thee, never can another possess my heart, never—

never—O God, why must one part from what one so loves, and yet my life in V. at present is a wretched life. Thy love has made me one of the happiest and, at the same time, one of the unhappiest of men—at my age I need a quiet, steady life—is that possible in our situation ? My Angel, I have just heard that the post goes every day, and I must therefore stop, so that you may receive the letter without delay. Be calm, only by calm consideration of our existence can we attain our aim to live together—be calm—love me—to-day—yesterday—what tearful longing after thee—thee—thee—my life—my all—farewell—Oh, continue to love me—never misjudge the faithful heart

Of Thy Beloved

L.

ever thine
ever mine
ever each other's.

Lord Byron

Caroline Lamb

Caroline Lamb had penned an accurate first impression of Lord Byron—mad, bad, and dangerous to know. Byron's fame, by then, had skyrocketed after Childe Harold's Pilgrimage had been published. They met each other in 1812 and Byron was instantly infatuated with her. He relentlessly pursued her, making her admit that she loved him more than she did her husband.

Byron was a womanizer and his passion dimmed soon after it had ignited. The courtship only lasted for two months.

August 1812

My dearest Caroline,

If tears, which you saw & know I am not apt to shed, if the agitation in which I parted from you, agitation which you must have perceived through the whole of this most nervous nervous affair, did not commence till the moment of leaving you approached, if all that I have said & done, & am still but too ready to say & do, have not sufficiently proved what my real feelings are & must be ever towards you, my love, I have no other proof to offer.

God knows I wish you happy, & when I quit you, or rather when you from a sense of duty to your husband & mother quit me, you shall acknowledge the truth of what I again promise & vow, that no other in word or deed shall ever hold the place in my affection which is & shall be most sacred to you, till I am nothing.

I never knew till that moment, the madness of—my dearest & most beloved friend—I cannot express myself—this is no time for words—but I shall have a pride, a melancholy pleasure, in suffering what you yourself can hardly conceive—for you dont not know me.—I am now about to go out with a heavy heart, because—my appearing this Evening will stop any absurd story which the events of today might give rise to—do you think now that I am cold & stern, & artful—will even others think so, will your mother even—that mother to whom we must indeed sacrifice much, more much more on my part, than she shall ever know or can imagine.

"Promises not to love you" ah Caroline it is past promising—but shall attribute all concessions to the proper motive—& never cease to feel all that you have already witnessed—& more than can ever be known but to my own heart—perhaps to yours—May God protect forgive & bless you—ever & even more than ever.

yr. most attached

BYRON

P.S.—These taunts which have driven you to this— my dearest Caroline—were it not for your mother & the kindness of all your connections, is there anything on earth or heaven would have made me so happy as to have made you mine long ago? & not less now than then, but more than ever at this time—you know I would with pleasure give up all here & all beyond the grave for you—& in refraining from this—must my motives be misunderstood?

I care not who knows this—what use is made of it—it is you & to you only that they owe yourself, I was and am yours, freely & most entirely, to obey, to honour, love & fly with you when, where, & how you yourself might & may determine.

FROM
Maria Branwell
TO
Patrick Bronte

Maria Branwell had moved to live with her aunt and uncle after her parents' death, hoping to start a new life at Rawdon, near Leeds. During one of her visits to a school where her uncle was headmaster, she met her future husband. The humble and charming curate of the nearby parish, Patrick Bronte was smitten when he first met the young and petite Maria. They had a brief but passionate courtship, and married each other by the end of the year 1812.

26 August 1812

My dear Friend,

This address is sufficient to convince you that I not only permit, but approve of yours to me—I do indeed consider you as my friend; yet when I consider how short a time I have had the pleasure of knowing you, I start at my own rashness, my heart fails, and did I not think that you would be disappointed and grieved, I believe I should be ready to spare myself the task of writing. Do not think I am so wavering as to repent of what I have already said. No, believe me, this will never be the case, unless you give me cause for it.

You need not fear that you have mistaken in my character. If I know anything of myself, I am incapable of making an ungenerous return to the smallest degree of kindness, much less to you whose attentions and conduct have been so particularly obliging. I will frankly confess that your behaviour and what I have seen and heard of your character has excited my warmest esteem and regard and be assured you shall never have cause to repent of any confidence you may think proper to place in me, and that it will always be my endeavour to deserve the good opinion which you have formed, although human weakness may in some instances cause me to fall short. In giving you these assurances I do not depend upon my own strength, but I look to him who has been my unerring guide through life, and in whose continued protection and assistance I confidently trust.

I thought on you much on Sunday, and feared you would not escape the rain. I hope you do not feel any bad effects from it? My cousin wrote you on Monday and expects this afternoon to be favoured with an answer. Your letter has caused me some foolish embarrassment, tho' in pity to my feelings they have been sparing of their raillery.

I will now candidly answer your questions. The politeness of others can never make me forget your kind attentions, neither can I walk our accustomed rounds without thinking on you, and, why should I be ashamed to add, wishing for your presence. If you knew what were my feelings whilst writing this you would pity me. I wish to write the truth and give you satisfaction, yet fear to go too far, and exceed the bounds of propriety. But whatever I may say or write I will never deceive you, or exceed the truth. If you think I have not placed the utmost confidence in you, consider my situation, and as yourself if I have not confided in you sufficiently, perhaps too much. I am very sorry that you will not have this till after tomorrow, but it was out of my power to write sooner. I rely on your goodness to pardon everything in this which may appear either too free or too stiff, and beg that you will consider me as a warm and faithful friend.

My uncle, aunt, and cousin unite in kind regards.

I must now conclude with again declaring myself to be

yours sincerely,
Maria Branwell

Mary Shelley

P B Shelley

Mary Godwin was seventeen when she first met P B Shelley. She fell for this young, eloquent, rebellious poet and the two often met secretly at Mary's mother's grave. But their match was opposed by Mary's father, and Percy's friend, William Godwin. Percy was married to Harriet at the time, and had sought financial help from William but had been unable, or unwilling, to pay him back. Determined to be with her, Percy eloped with Mary, leaving his daughter and pregnant wife behind.

25 October 1814

For what a minute did I see you yesterday—is this the way my beloved that we are to live till the sixth in the morning I look for you and when I awake I turn to look on you—dearest Shelley you are solitary and uncomfortable why cannot I be with you to cheer you and to press you to my heart oh my love you have no friends why then should you be torn from the only one who has affection for you— But I shall see you tonight and that is the hope that I shall live on through the day– be happy dear Shelley and think of me—why do I say this dearest & only one I know how tenderly you love me and how you repine at this absence from me—when shall we be free from fear of treachery?

I send you the letter I told you of from Harriet and a letter we received yesterday from fanny the history of this interview I will tell you when I come—but perhaps as it is so rainy a day Fanny will not be allowed to come at all—

My love my own one be happy—

I was so dreadfully tired yesterday that I was obliged to take a coach home forgive this extravagance but I am so very weak at present & I had been so agitated through the day that I was not able to stand a morning rest however will set me quite right again and I shall be quite well when I meet you this evening—will you be at the door of the coffee house at five o'clock as it is désagreable to go into those places and I shall be there exactly at the time & we will go into St. Pauls where we can sit down.

I send you Diogenes as you have no books—Hookham was so ill tempered as not to send the books I asked for.

P B Shelley

Mary Shelley

25 October 1814

I have written an extremely urgent letter to
Harriet to induce her to send money. I have
written also to Hookham, who did not call
upon Peacock. I have told Harriet that I shall
be at Pancras when her answer arrives. I shall
see you tonight, my beloved Mary, fear not.
I have confidence in the fortunate issue of
our distresses. I am desolate and wretched in
your absence; I feel disturbed and wild even to
conceive that we should be separated. But this
is most necessary, nor must we omit caution
even on our unfrequent meetings. Recollect

that I am lost if the people can have watched you to me. I wander restlessly about; I cannot read or even write; but this will soon pass. I should not inflict my own Mary with my dejection; she has sufficient cause for disturbance to need consolation from me. Well, we shall meet today. I cannot write, but I love you with so unalterable love that the contemplation of me will serve for a letter. If you see Hookham, do not insult him openly; I have still hopes. We must not resign an inch of hope. I will make this remorseless villain loathe his own flesh in good time; he shall be cut down in his season; his pride shall be trampled into atoms; I will wither up his selfish soul by piecemeal.

Claire Clairmont

Lord Byron

Claire Clairmont was happy when she had managed to seduce the famous poet and womanizer, Lord Byron. He was, at the time, in the final stages of getting a divorce. But Claire's happiness was short-lived. Like many of the women in Byron's life, he soon got bored of Claire as well.

Claire, determined to get him back, travelled with her stepsister Mary Shelley and her husband P B Shelley, to Geneva where Byron was residing. Byron gave a warm welcome to the Shelleys but chose to ignore the woman accompanying them. Claire was pregnant with his child at the time, but Byron was still apathetic. P B Shelley had to coerce Byron to promise to provide for the child.

Claire remained bitter till the end. At the age 70, in her memoirs, this was what she wrote of

Byron—'a human tiger slaking his thirst for inflicting pain upon defenceless women.'

1815

You bid me write short to you and I have much to say. You also bade me believe that it was a fancy which made me cherish an attachment for you. It cannot be a fancy since you have been for the last year the object upon which every solitary moment led me to muse.

I do not expect you to love me, I am not worthy of your love. I feel you are superior, yet much to my surprise, more to my happiness, you betrayed passions I had believed no longer alive in your bosom. Shall I also have to ruefully experience the want of happiness? Shall I reject it when it is offered? I may appear to you imprudent, vicious; my opinions detestable, my theory depraved; but one thing, at least, time shall show you: that I love gently and with affection, that I am incapable of anything approaching to the feeling of revenge or malice; I do assure you, your future will shall be mine, and everything you shall do or say, I shall not question.

Have you then any objection to the following plan? On Thursday Evening we may go out of town together by some stage or mail about the distance of ten or twelve miles. There we shall be free and unknown; we can return early the following morning. I have arranged everything here so that slightest suspicion may not be excited. Pray do so with your people.

Will you admit me for two moments to settle with you where? Indeed I will not stay an instant after you tell me to go. Only so much may be said and done in a short time by an interview which writing cannot effect. Do what you will, or go where you will, refuse to see me and behave unkindly, I shall never forget you. I shall ever remember the gentleness of your manners and the wild originality of your countenance. Having been once seen, you are not to be forgotten. Perhaps this is the last time I shall ever address you. Once more, then, let me assure you that I am not ungrateful. In all things have you acted most honourably, and I am only provoked that the awkwardness of my manner and something like timidity has hitherto prevented my expressing it to you personally.

Clara Clairmont

Lord Byron

Annabella Milbanke

People had understood that things were not well between Lord and Lady Byron when the man went around calling his wife a 'moral Clytemnestra'.

Byron had proposed to Annabella Milbanke twice. Though rejected at first, she eventually gave in and the two got married in 1815. But Byron's sexual escapades didn't stop. Unable to tolerate her husband's infidelity, Annabella legally separated from him and went to live with her parents in 1816. During this time, aspersions on Byron's characters were also being made due to his incestuous relationship with his half-sister, Augusta Leigh. He left England in the same year, and never returned.

February 8, 1816

All I can say seems useless—and all I could say
might be no less unavailing—yet I still cling to the
wreck of my hopes, before they sink for ever. Were
you, then, never happy with me? Did you never
at any time or times express yourself so? Have
no marks of affection of the warmest and most
reciprocal attachment passed between us? or did in
fact hardly a day go down without some such on
one side, and generally on both? Do not mistake
me: I have not denied my state of mind—but you
know its causes—and were those deviations from
calmness never followed by acknowledgements and
repentance? Was not the last that recurred more
particularly so? and had I not—had we not the days
before and on the day we parted—every reason to
believe that we loved each other? that we were to
meet again? Were not your letters kind? Had I not
acknowledged to you all my faults and follies—and
assured you that some had not and could not be
repeated? I do not require these questions to be
answered to me, but to your own heart. It is torture
to correspond thus, and there are things to be settled
and said which cannot be written.

   You say it is my disposition to deem what I
have worthless? Did I deem you so? Did I ever so

express myself to you, or of you to others? You are much changed within these twenty days or you would never have thus poisoned your own better feelings and trampled on mine.

Ever your most truly and affectly.

B.

John Keats

Fanny Brawne

It was 1872. Edmund, Herbert, and Margaret huddled around the love letters. They had promised their late mother, Francis Lindon, that they will never tell their father about them. All their father had known was that John Keats and their mother had been neighbours in Hampstead. But Louis Lindon was dead now. Finally, the children could profit from their mother's secret love story.

Causing a furore at the time of their publication, these letters were a revelation. The renowned John Keats was not only a poet but also a hopeless romantic.

Newport

July 3, 1819

Shanklin, Isle of Wight, Thursday

My dearest Lady—I am glad I had not an opportunity of sending off a Letter which I wrote for you on Tuesday night—'twas too much like one out of Rousseau's Heloise. I am more reasonable this morning. The morning is the only proper time for me to write to a beautiful Girl whom I love so much: for at night, when the lonely day has closed, and the lonely, silent, unmusical Chamber is waiting to receive me as into a Sepulchre, then believe me my passion gets entirely the sway, then I would not have you see those Rhapsodies which I once thought it impossible I should ever give way to, and which I have often laughed at in another, for fear you should [think me] either too unhappy or perhaps a little mad.

I am now at a very pleasant Cottage window, looking onto a beautiful hilly country, with a glimpse of the sea; the morning is very fine. I do not know how elastic my spirit might be, what pleasure I might have in living here and breathing and wandering as free as a stag about this beautiful Coast if the remembrance of you did not weigh so upon me I have never known any unalloy'd Happiness for many days together: the death or sickness of some one has always spoilt my hours—and now when none such troubles oppress me, it is you must confess very hard that another sort of pain should haunt me.

Ask yourself my love whether you are not very cruel to have so entrammelled me, so destroyed my freedom. Will you confess this in the Letter you must write immediately, and do all you can to console me in it—make it rich as a draught of poppies to intoxicate me—write the softest words and kiss them that I may at least touch my lips where yours have been. For myself I know not how to express my devotion to so fair a form: I want a brighter word than bright, a fairer word than fair. I almost wish we were butterflies and liv'd but three summer days—three such days with you I could fill with more delight than fifty common years could ever contain. But however selfish I may feel, I am sure I could never act selfishly: as I told you a day or two before I left Hampstead, I will never return to London if my Fate does not turn up Pam or at least a Court-card. Though I could centre my Happiness in you, I cannot expect to engross your heart so entirely—indeed if I thought you felt as much for me as I do for you at this moment I do not think I could restrain myself from seeing you again tomorrow for the delight of one embrace.

But no—I must live upon hope and Chance. In case of the worst that can happen, I shall still love you—but what hatred shall I have for another!

Some lines I read the other day are continually ringing a peal in my ears:

> To see those eyes I prize above mine
>   own
> Dart favors on another—
> And those sweet lips (yielding
>   immortal nectar)
> Be gently press'd by any but myself—
> Think, think Francesca, what a cursed
>   thing
> It were beyond expression!

J.

Do write immediately. There is no Post from this Place, so you must address Post Office, Newport, Isle of Wight. I know before night I shall curse myself for having sent you so cold a Letter; yet it is better to do it as much in my senses as possible. Be as kind as the distance will permit to your

J. Keats

Present my Compliments to your mother, my love to Margaret and best remembrances to your Brother—if you please so.

July 8, 1819

My sweet Girl—Your Letter gave me more delight than any thing in the world but yourself could do; indeed I am almost astonished that any absent one should have that luxurious power over my senses which I feel. Even when I am not thinking of you I receive your influence and a tenderer nature stealing upon me. All my thoughts, my unhappiest days and nights have I find not at all cured me of my love of Beauty, but made it so intense that I am miserable that you are not with me: or rather breathe in that dull sort of patience that cannot be called Life.

I never knew before, what such a love as you have made me feel, was; I did not believe in it; my Fancy was afraid of it, lest it should burn me up. But if you will fully love me, though there may be some fire, 'twill not be more than we can bear when moistened and bedewed with Pleasures.

You mention 'horrid people' and ask me whether it depend upon them whether I see you again. Do understand me, my love, in this. I have so much of you in my heart that I must turn Mentor when I see a chance of harm befalling you. I would never see any thing but Pleasure in your eyes, love on your lips, and Happiness in your steps. I would wish to see you among those amusements suitable to your inclinations and spirits; so that our loves might be a delight in the midst of Pleasures agreeable enough, rather than a resource from vexations and cares. But I doubt much, in case of the worst, whether I shall be philosopher enough to follow my own Lessons: if I saw my resolution give you a pain I could not.

Why may I not speak of your Beauty, since without that I could never have lov'd you? I cannot conceive any beginning of such love as I have for you but Beauty. There may be a sort of love for which, without the least sneer at it, I have the highest respect and can admire it in others: but it has not the richness, the bloom, the full form, the enchantment of love after my own heart. So let me speak of your Beauty, though to my own endangering; if you could be so cruel to me as to try elsewhere its Power.

You say you are afraid I shall think you do not love me—in saying this you make me ache the more to be near you. I am at the diligent use of my faculties here, I do not pass a day without sprawling some blank verse or tagging some rhymes; and here

I must confess, that, (since I am on that subject,) I love you the more in that I believe you have liked me for my own sake and for nothing else. I have met with women whom I really think would like to be married to a Poem and to be given away by a Novel. I have seen your Comet, and only wish it was a sign that poor Rice would get well whose illness makes him rather a melancholy companion: and the more so as so to conquer his feelings and hide them from me, with a forc'd Pun.

I kiss'd your Writing over in the hope you had indulg'd me by leaving a trace of honey. What was your dream? Tell it me and I will tell you the interpretation thereof.

Ever yours, my love!

Do not accuse me of delay—we have not here any opportunity of sending letters every day. Write speedily.

July 27, 1819

Sunday Night

My sweet Girl—I hope you did not blame me much for not obeying your request of a Letter on Saturday: we have had four in our small room playing at cards night and morning leaving me no undisturb'd opportunity to write. Now Rice and Martin are gone I am at liberty. Brown to my sorrow confirms the account you give of your ill health. You cannot conceive how I ache to be with you: how I would die for one hour—for what is in the world? I say you cannot conceive; it is impossible you should look with such eyes upon me as I have upon you: it cannot be.

Forgive me if I wander a little this evening, for I have been all day employ'd in a very abstract Poem and I am in deep love with you two things which must excuse me. I have, believe me, not been an age in letting you take possession of me; the very first week I knew you I wrote myself your vassal; but burnt the Letter as the very next time I saw you I thought you manifested some dislike to me. If you should ever feel for Man at the first sight what I did for you, I am lost. Yet I should not quarrel with you, but hate myself if such a thing were to happen— only I should burst if the thing were not as fine as a Man as you are as a Woman.

Perhaps I am too vehement, then fancy me on my knees, especially when I mention a part of your Letter which hurt me; you say speaking of Mr. Severn 'but you must be satisfied in knowing that I admired you much more than your friend.' My dear love, I cannot believe there ever was or ever could be any thing to admire in me especially as far as sight goes—I cannot be admired, I am not a thing to be admired. You are, I love you; all I can bring you is a swooning admiration of your Beauty. I hold that place among Men which snub-nos'd brunettes with meeting eyebrows do among women—they are trash to me—unless I should find one among them with a fire in her heart like the one that burns in mine.

You absorb me in spite of myself—you alone: for I look not forward with any pleasure to what is called being settled in the world; I tremble at domestic cares—yet for you I would meet them, though if it would leave you the happier I would rather die than do so.

I have two luxuries to brood over in my walks, your Loveliness and the hour of my death. O that I could have possession of them both in the same minute. I hate the world: it batters too much the wings of my self-will, and would I could take a sweet poison from your lips to send me out of it. From no others would I take it. I am indeed astonish'd to find myself so careless of all charms but yours—remembering as I do the time when even a bit of ribband was a matter of interest with me.

What softer words can I find for you after this—
what it is I will not read. Nor will I say more here,
but in a Postscript answer any thing else you may
have mentioned in your Letter in so many words—
for I am distracted with a thousand thoughts. I will
imagine you Venus tonight and pray, pray, pray to
your star like a Heathen.

Your's ever, fair Star,

John Keats

⁓⊙⊙⁓

13 October 1819

My dearest Girl,

This moment I have set myself to copy some
verses out fair. I cannot proceed with any degree
of content. I must write you a line or two and see if
that will assist in dismissing you from my Mind for
ever so short a time. Upon my Soul I can think of
nothing else—The time is passed when I had power
to advise and warn you again[s]t the unpromising
morning of my Life—My love has made me selfish.
I cannot exist without you—I am forgetful of every
thing but seeing you again—my Life seems to stop

there—I see no further. You have absorb'd me. I have a sensation at the present moment as though I was dissolving—I should be exquisitely miserable without the hope of soon seeing you. I should be afraid to separate myself far from you. My sweet Fanny, will your heart never change? My love, will it? I have no limit now to my love—You note came in just here—I cannot be happier away from you— 'Tis richer than an Argosy of Pearles. Do not threat me even in jest. I have been astonished that Men could die Martyrs for religion—I have shudder'd at it—I shudder no more—I could be martyr'd for my Religion—Love is my religion—I could die for that—I could die for you. My Creed is Love and you are its only tenet—You have ravish'd me away by a Power I cannot resist: and yet I could resist till I saw you; and even since I have seen you I have endeavoured often 'to reason against the reasons of my Love'. I can do that no more—the pain would be too great—My Love is selfish—I cannot breathe without you.

Yours for ever
John Keats

March 1820

Sweetest Fanny

You fear, sometimes, I do not love you so much as you wish? My dear Girl I love you ever and ever and without reserve. The more I have known you the more have I lov'd. In every way—even my jealousies have been agonies of Love, in the hottest fit I ever had I would have died for you. I have vex'd you too much. But for Love! Can I help it? You are always new. The last of your kisses was ever the sweetest; the last smile the brightest; the last movement the gracefullest. When you pass'd my window home yesterday, I was fill'd with as much admiration as if I had then seen you for the first time. You uttered half complaint once that I only lov'd your Beauty. Have I nothing else then to love in you but that? Do not I see a heart naturally furnish'd with wings imprison itself with me? No ill prospect has been able to turn your thoughts a moment from me. This perhaps should be as much a subject of sorrow as of joy—but I will not talk of that. Even if you did not love me I could not help an entire devotion to you: how much more deeply then must I feel for you knowing you love me. My Mind has been the most discontented and restless one that ever was put into a body too small for it. I never felt my Mind repose upon anything with complete and undistracted enjoyment—upon no person but you. When you are in the room my thoughts never fly out of window: you always concentrate my whole senses. The anxiety shown about our Loves in your last note is an immense pleasure to me: however you must not suffer such speculations to molest you any more: nor will I any more believe you can have the least pique against me. Brown is gone out—but here is Mrs Wylie—when she is gone I shall be awake for you.——Remembrances to your Mother.

Your affectionate
J. Keats

8 August 1820

> I do not write this till the last
> that no eye may catch it.

My dearest Girl,

I wish you could invent some means to make me at all happy without you. Every hour I am more concentrated in you; every thing else tastes like chaff in my Mouth. I feel it almost impossible to go to Italy—the fact is I cannot leave you, and shall never taste one minute's content until it pleases chance to let me live with you for good. But I will not go on at this rate. A person in health as you are can have no conception of the horrors that nerves and a temper like mine go through. What Island do your friends propose retiring to? I should be happy to go with you there alone, but in company I should object to it; the backbitings and jealousies of new colonists who have nothing else to amuse themselves, is unbearable. Mr. Dilke came to see me yesterday, and gave me a very great deal more pain than pleasure. I shall never be able any more to endure to for the society of any of those who used to meet at Elm Cottage and Wentorth Place. The last two years taste like brass upon my Palate. If I cannot live with you I will live alone. I do not think my health will improve much while I am separated from you. For all this I am averse to seeing you—I cannot bear flashes of light and return into my glooms again. I am not so unhappy with you seems such an impossibility! It requires a luckier star than mine! It will never be. I enclose a passage from one of your letters which I want you to alter a little—I want (if you will have it so) the matter expressed less coldly to me. If my health would bear it, I could write a Poem which I have in my head, which would be a consolation for people in such a situation as mine. I would show some one in Love as I am, with a person living in such Liberty as you do. Shakespeare always sums up matters in the most sovereign manner. Hamlet's heart was full of such Misery as mine is when he said to Ophelia "go to a Nunnery, go, go". Indeed I should like to give up the matter at once—I should like to die. I am sickened at the brute world which you are smiling with. I hate men and women more. I see nothing but thorns for the future—wherever I may be next winter in Italy or nowhere Brown will be living near you with his indecencies—I see no prospect of any rest. Suppose me in Rome—well, I should there see you as in a magic glass going to and from town at all hours,—I wish you could infuse a little confidence in human nature into my heart. I cannot muster any—the world is too brutal for me—I am glad there is such a thing as the grave—I am sure I shall never have any rest till I get there At any rate I will indulge myself by never seeing any more Dilke or Brown or any of their Friends. I wish I was either in your arms full of faith or that a Thunder bolt would strike me.

God bless you.

J.K

Lord Byron

Countess Guicciola

Byron met Teresa in the autumn of 1818. She was a beautiful girl of eighteen, and was about to be married to the sixty-year-old Count Guicciola. Their union was impossible but that did not stop either of them from loving each other. One day, when Teresa was not at home, Byron sat in her garden and read her copy of Corianne. He left the following letter on one of the fly-leaves of the book.

Bologna, Aug. 25, 1819.

My dearest Teresa,—I have read this book in your garden. My love, you were absent, or else I could not have read it. It is a favourite book of yours, and the writer was a friend of mine. You will not understand these English words, and others will not understand them, which is the reason I have not scrawled them in Italian; but you will recognize the handwriting of him who passionately loved you, and you will divine that over a book which was yours he could only think of love. In that word, beautiful in all languages, but most so in yours,— Amor mio,—is comprised my existence here and hereafter.

I feel I exist here, and I fear that I shall exist hereafter—to what purpose you will decide; my destiny rests with you, and you are a woman, eighteen years of age, and two out of a convent. I wish that you had stayed there, with all my heart,— or, at least, that I had never met you in your married state.

But all this is too late. I love you and you love me,—at least, you say so and act as if you did so, which last is a great consolation in all events. But I more than love you, and cannot cease to love you.

Think of me sometimes when the Alps and the ocean divide us; but they never will, unless you wish it.

Byron.

William Hazlitt

Sarah Walker

William Hazlitt was renting a room at a lodging house in Chancery Lane, London, when Sarah Walker came in the room with his breakfast. Hazlitt was instantly besotted with her. He was all set to marry her, but Sarah was just passing the time.

She soon fell for another lodger. Hazlitt tried to win her back, but it was not meant to be.

March 1822.

You will be glad to learn that I have done my work,—a volume in less than a month. That is one reason why I am better than when I came; and another is, I have had two letters from Sarah.

I walk out of an afternoon and hear the birds sing, as I told you, and think if I had you hanging on my arm, and that for life, how happy I should be, happier than I ever hoped to be, or had any conception of till I knew you. "But that can never be," I hear you answer in a soft, low murmur. Well, let me dream of it sometimes. I am not happy too often, except when that favourite note, the harbinger of spring, recalling the hopes of my youth, whispers thy name and peace together in my ear. I was reading something about Mr. Macready today, and this puts me in mind of that delicious night when I went with your mother and you to see 'Romeo and Juliet.' Can I forget it for a moment?—our sweet, modest looks, your infinite propriety of behaviour, all your sweet, winning ways, your hesitating about taking my arm, as we came out, till your mother did, your laughing about nearly losing your cloak, your stepping into the coach, and oh, my sitting down beside you there,—you, whom I had loved so long, so well,—and your assuring me I had not lessened your pleasure at the play by being with you, and giving me your dear hand to press in mine!

I thought I was in heaven! That slender form contained my all of heaven upon earth; and as I folded you—yes, you, my own Sarah—to my bosom, there was, as you say, a tie between us. You did seem to me, for those few short moments, to be mine in all truth, honour, and sacred ness. Oh that we could be always so! Do not mock me, for I am a very child in love. I ought to beg pardon for behaving so ill afterwards, but I hope the little image made it all up between us.

Jane Welsh

Thomas Carlyle

Jane Welsh's tutor and former suitor had been the one to introduce her to her future husband, the essayist Thomas Carlyle. They married in 1826, and the marriage was nothing short of a rollercoaster ride.

All was good till Carlyle became infatuated with another woman, who was also married. She regularly sent him invitations to her house, and he was more than happy to accept. The affair came to an end when the other woman died in 1857, and Jane managed to spend some calm years with her husband.

Haddington,
6th September 1823.

My dear friend,

Your Letter only reached me this morning, I
having sojourned at Templand more than ten days,
'expecting an opportunity'. Charming as it is, I
could almost wish it had not cast up at all, for it has
troubled me more than I can tell. I feel there is need
I should answer it without delay. And what can I
say to you? It is so hard to explain oneself in such
a situation! But I must, and in plain terms; for any
reserve at present were criminal and might be very
fatal in its consequences to us both.

You misunderstand me. You regard me no
longer as a Friend, a Sister, but as one who at some
future period may be more to you than both. Is it
not so? Is it not true that you believe me, like the
bulk of my silly sex, incapable of entertaining a
strong affection for a man of my own age without
having for its ultimate object our union for life?
'Useless and dangerous to love you!' 'My happiness
wrecked by you!' I cannot have misinterpreted your
meaning! And, my God! what have I said or done
to mislead you into an error so destructive to the
confidence that subsists betwixt us, so dangerous

to the peace of both? In my treatment of you, I have indeed disregarded all maxims of womanly prudence; have shaken myself free from the shackles of etiquette; I have loved and admired you for your noble qualities, and for the extraordinary affection you have shown me; and I have told you so without reserve or disguise; but not till out repeated quarrels had produced an explanation betwixt us, which I foolishly believed would guarantee my future conduct from all possibility of misconstruction. I have been to blame. I might have foreseen that such implicit confidence might mislead you as to the nature of my sentiments, and should have expressed my friendship for you with a more prudent reserve. But it is of no use talking of what I might or should have done in the time past. I have only to repair the mischief in as far as I can, now that my eyes are opened to it, now that I am startled to find our relation actually assuming the aspect of an engagement for life. My Friend, I love you. I repeat it, tho' I find the expression a rash one. All the best feelings of my nature are concerned in loving you. But were you my Brother I would love you the same; were I married to another I would love you the same, And is this sentiment so calm, so delightful, but so unimpassioned, enough to recompense the freedom of my heart, enough to reconcile me to the existence of a married woman, the hopes and wishes and ambitions of which are all so different from mine, the cares and occupations of which are my disgust! Oh no! Your Friend I will be, your truest most devoted Friend, while I breathe the breath of life; but your Wife! Never, never! not though you were as rich as Croesus, as honoured and as renowned as you yet shall be.

You may think I am viewing the matter by much too seriously; taking fright when there is nothing to fear. It is well if it be so! But suffering as I am at this very moment from the horrid pain of seeing a true and affectionate heart near breaking for my sake, it is not to be wondered at tho' I be over-anxious for your peace on which my own depends in a still greater degree. Write to me and reassure me, for God's sake if you can! Your friendship at this time is almost necessary to my existence. Yet I will resign it cost what it may, will, will resign it, if it can only be enjoyed at the risk of your future peace. I had many things to say to you, about Musaus and all that; but I must wait till another opportunity. At present I scarcely know what I am about.

Ever affectionately yours,

JANE B. WELSH.

Balzac

Ewelina Hanska (edited)

Balzac fervently exchanged letters with his beloved Countess Hanska. They had only met twice but his love for her knew no bounds. Both of them decided to marry once the Count was dead. However, Balzac's financial problems posed a problem and he couldn't marry her before 1850. They spent short, but blissful, five months with each other.

October 13, 1833

Oh! darling, you are adorably loving, but how stupid you are to have fears. No, no, my cherished Eva, I am not one of those who punish a woman for her love. Oh! I would I could remain half a day at your knees, my head on your knees, telling you my thoughts lazily, with delight, saying nothing sometimes, but kissing your gown. Mon Dieu! how sweet would be the day when I could play at liberty with you, as a child with its mother. O my beloved Eva, day of my days, light of my nights, my hope, my adored, my all-beloved, my sole darling, when can I see you? Is it an illusion? Have I seen you? Have I seen you enough to say that I have seen you?

Mon Dieu! how I love your rather broad accent, your mouth of kindness, of voluptuousness—permit me to say it to you, my angel of love!

I work night and day to go and see you for a fortnight in December. I shall cross the Jura covered with snow, but I shall think of the snowy shoulders of my love, my well-beloved. Ah! to breathe your hair, to hold your hand, to strain you in my arms! that's where my courage comes from. I have friends here who are stupefied at the fierce will I am displaying at this moment. Ah! they don't know my darling, my soft darling, her, whose mere sight robs pain of its stings! Yes, Parisina and her lover must have died without feeling the axe, as they thought of one another!

A kiss, my angel of earth, a kiss tasted slowly. Adieu. The nightingale has sung too long; I am allured to write to you, and Eugénie Grandet scolds.

Juliette Drouet

Victor Hugo

Victor Hugo met Juliette Drouet at a time when he was in deep despair. His wife and childhood sweetheart, Adele had betrayed him. Juliette Drouet was a coquette; she had had many lovers before Hugo. A famous actress, she was more beautiful than talented.

Their love affair started in 1833, and soon after Juliette began living at Les Metz. It was a hamlet near Victor Hugo's house, where he lived with Adele. Juliette and Victor would often meet halfway between both houses, near a chestnut tree, leaving each other notes, letters, and poems.

Though their relationship was not without its fair share of arguments, they were together for the rest of their lives, till Juliette died in 1883.

1833

Sunday, 8.30 p.m.

Before beginning to copy or count words, I must write you one line of love, my dear little lunatic. I love you—do you understand, I love you! This is a profession of faith which comprises all my duty and integrity. I love you, ergo, I am faithful to you, I see only you, think only of you, speak only to you, touch only you, breathe you, desire you, dream of you; in a word, I love you! that means everything.

Do not therefore give way any more to melancholy; permit yourself to be loved and to be happy. Fear nothing from me, never doubt me, and we shall be blissful beyond words.

I am expecting you shortly, and am ready with warm and tender caresses which, I hope, will cheer you.

Your Juju.

1833

Wednesday, 2.30 p.m.

I cannot refrain, dearly beloved, from commenting upon the profound melancholy you were in this morning, and upon the doubt you manifest on every occasion as to the sincerity of my love. This unjustifiable suspicion on your part disheartens me beyond all expression. It intimidates me and makes me fear to confide to you the incidents my dubious position exposes me to. Today, for instance, I concealed from you the visit of a creditor, who presented himself to the porter, but was not shown up. I paid him out of my own resources, without your knowledge, because you are always telling me I do not love you. This expression from you makes me feel that you hold a shameful opinion of me and my character, rendered possible perhaps by my situation, but none the less false, unjust, and cruel.

I love you because I love you, because it would be impossible for me not to love you. I love you without question, without calculation, without reason good or bad, faithfully, with all my heart and soul, and every faculty. Believe it, for it is true. If you cannot believe, I being at your side, I will make a drastic effort to force you to do so. I shall have the mournful satisfaction of sacrificing myself utterly to a distrust as absurd as it is unfounded.

Meanwhile, I ask your pardon for the guilty thought that came to me this morning, and which may possibly recur, if you continue to see in my love only a mean-spirited compliance and an unworthy speculation. This letter is very lengthy, and very sad to write. I trust with all my soul, that I may never have to reiterate its sentiments.

I love you. Indeed I love you. Believe in me.

Juliette.

ↄ◦◎◦ↄ

1833

Wednesday, 2 a.m.

My Victor,

I love you truly, and neither know, nor can conceive, any personality more deserving of devotion than yourself.

I look up to you as a faithful, reliable friend, as the noblest and most estimable of men.

It hurts me to feel that my past life must be an obstacle to your confidence. Before I cared for you, I felt no shame for it, I made no attempt to conceal or alter it; but, since I have known you, this attitude of mind has changed in every respect. I blush for myself, and dread lest my love have not the strength to erase the stains of the past. I fear it even more, when you suspect me unjustly.

My Victor, it is for your love to sanctify me, for your esteem to renew in me all that once was good and pure.

I care for you so much that all this is possible. I will become worthy of you, if you will only help me.

Farewell. You are my soul, my life, my religion; I love you.

Juliette.

1833

It is not quite six o'clock in the evening. I have just finished copying the verses you gave me yesterday. I am not very familiar with the forms of compliment in usage in fashionable society. All I can tell you is that I wept and admired when I heard you read them, that I wept and admired when I read them to myself, and that once more I weep and admire in recalling them. I thank you from the bottom of my heart for having thought of me when you were writing them. Thank you, my beloved, for the benign sentiments that inspired you. Your beautiful lines have had the effect you anticipated, for they have acted both as a cordial and a sedative to my sick spirit. Thank you! thank you! and again, thank you! You are not only sublime—you are kind, and, what is better still, you are indulgent, you who have so much right to be severe.

I love you. My heart melts in admiration and adoration. There is more rapture of love in my poor bosom than it is capable of containing. Come then, and receive the superabundance of my ecstasy.

If you only knew how I long for you, and desire you! If you knew more still, you would come, I am very sure! Come, come, I beg you, come! You shall have a kiss for every step, a recompense for every effort, more smiles, and more joy, than you will encounter fog and cold.

Juliette.

December 20th, 1833

My beloved Victor,

I have been very unjust to you. You have had cause to call me ungrateful and unworthy. You will soon hate me—soon also, you will have forgotten me. I feel it. You see, there can be no thought or sentiment of yours that I do not understand and apprehend. At this moment, even while I am writing to you, you are blaming me for suffering. You are annoyed with me for idolising you with an extravagance which renders me mad and jealous. You are tired of my love. It cramps you, fatigues you. You meditate flying from me. My bad luck frightens you; you fear to share it longer. You dread the responsibility—say, rather, you love me less, perhaps not at all. Oh, what suffering that fear gives me! My head is aching. I wish I could die. It must be my fault. I have been wrong to show you the hideous wound in my heart, the jealousy which lacerates and destroys it. Yes, I ought to have concealed my sufferings from you. I ought never to fly into those rages that betray the depth of my love and grief.

My Victor, do not leave me! I beg you on my knees, not to be daunted before a public responsibility. Who has the right to demand from you an account of the measure of the sacrifices you have made for me? What does it matter if you are denied the justice you deserve? What matter that you should be held responsible in part for my troubles? The point to be considered before all others, is your private relations with me. The responsibility you must accept is towards me only; it concerns only our two selves. If you repudiate it, it will kill me, for my whole life is wrapped up in you and your presence. I breathe only through your lips, see only with your eyes, live only in your heart. If you withdraw yourself from me, I must die.

Reflect! This is not a threat, to keep you near me. I am not exaggerating the extent to which you are necessary to my very existence—I am only telling you what I feel. It is the truth, but the truth under restriction, for I hardly dare acknowledge it in its entirety, even to myself. I need you! Only you! I cannot exist without you. Think of it. Try to love me enough to accept the charge of my life, with all its attendant bad luck.

Juliette.

1835

Friday, 8 p.m.

If only I were a clever woman, I could describe to you my gorgeous bird, how you unite in yourself the beauties of form, plumage, and song!

I would tell you that you are the greatest marvel of all ages, and I should only be speaking the simple truth. But to put all this into suitable words, my superb one, I should require a voice far more harmonious than that which is bestowed upon my species—for I am the humble owl that you mocked at only lately, therefore, it cannot be.

I will not tell you to what degree you are dazzling and to the birds of sweet song who, as you know, are none the less beautiful and appreciative.

I am content to delegate to them the duty of watching, listening and admiring, while to myself I reserve the right of loving; this may be less attractive to the ear, but it is sweeter far to the heart.

I love you, I love you. My Victor; I can not reiterate it too often; I can never express it as much as I feel it.

I recognise you in all the beauty that surrounds me in form, in colour, in perfume, in harmonious sound: all of these mean you to me. You are superior to all. I see and admire—you are all!

You are not only the solar spectrum with the seven luminous colours, but the sun himself, that illumines, warms, and revivifies! This is what you are, and I am the lowly woman that adores you.

Juliette

Alfred de Musset
George Sand

George Sand was thirty when she met the handsome and reputable writer, Alfred de Musset. She fell in love with this man who was seven years younger than her. At the time, Sand had become infamous for her stringent feministic ideals. She was considered amoral since she smoked, cross-dressed, and had had numerous lovers.

Musset's mother was furious when she heard about their affair—the disreputable woman was taking advantage of her naïve son. Nevertheless, Sand and Musset stayed together and even decided to take go on a little trip. Nothing went as planned though since Musset got sick when they reached Venice. A doctor was called.

Pietro Pagello did his job and went on his way, but not before stealing Sand's heart. He was her next lover.

1833

I have something stupid and ridiculous to tell you. I am foolishly writing to you instead of having told you this, I do not know why, when returning from that walk.

Tonight I shall be annoyed at having done so. You will laugh in my face, will take me for a maker of phrases in all my relations with you hitherto. You will show me the door and you will think I am lying.

I am in love with you. I have been thus since the first day I called on you.

Alfred de Musset

❧

Geneva, April 5th, 1834.

My beloved George, I am at Geneva. I left Milan without having found a letter of yours at the post. Perhaps you have written to me, but I booked our places in advance, as by chance the post from Venice, that usually arrives two hours before the departure of the coach to Geneva, was, this time, much delayed. I beg you, if you have written to me at Milan, to write the Postmaster there to forward your letter to Paris. I want it, if it is only two lines. Write to me at Paris, my love, I left you very fatigued, very exhausted from those two months of sorrow; besides, you have told me that you have much to say to me. Above all tell me that you are tranquil, that you are happy. You know that I supported the journey very well, Antonio will have told you that. I am strong, well, almost happy. Shall I tell you that I have not suffered, that I have not very often wept in those sad nights spent in inns? To do so would be to boast myself a brute and you would not believe that of me. I still love you passionately, George. In four days there will be three hundred leagues between us, so why should I not speak to you frankly? At this distance there can be no more violence or attacks of nerves; I love you, I know that you are with a man whom you love and yet I am calm. While I write tears stream over my hands, but they are the sweetest, the dearest tears that I have ever shed. I am calm; it is not a child exhausted from fatigue that talks thus to you. I declare that the sun in its orbit is no brighter than that light I have in my heart. I did not want to write to you until I was sure of myself, so many things have passed through this poor head! I awaken from such a strange dream. This morning I hastened through the street of Geneva, gazing into the shops; a new waistcoat, a fine edition of an English book—these attracted my attention. Chancing to see myself in a mirror, I recognised the child that I once was. What have you done, my poor friend? Was this the man that you wanted to love! Your heart was saddened with ten years of suffering, for ten years you had longed for happiness, and I was the reed on which you leant! You to love me! My poor George, that makes me tremble. I have made you so unhappy! And what greater miseries was I not about to cause you! I shall see it for a long time, my George, that face blanched by the watches spent beside my couch! I shall for a long time see you in that fatal chamber where so many tears have been shed.

Poor George! Poor dear child! You deceived yourself; you believed that you were my mistress, and you were only my mother; heaven made us, one for the other; our minds met in their elevated sphere, and recognising one another like the mountain birds, flew towards one another, but the embrace was too powerful; we committed incest. Oh, well, my only love, I have been as a tormentor for you, at least recently, I have made you suffer so much, but God be praised, what I might have done that would have been worse still, that I did not do. Oh, my child, you live, you are beautiful, you are young, you are under the most beautiful sky in the world, leaning on a man that has a heart worthy of you. Splendid young man! Tell him how much I like him and that I cannot restrain my tears in thinking of him. Ah, well, I have not cheated Providence, I have not turned from you the hand that you needed for your happiness to clasp! In leaving you I did perhaps the simplest thing in the world, but my heart dilates—despite my tears—to think that I have done it. I took with me two strange companions—sorrow and a limitless joy. When you pass the Simplon, George, think of me. It was there that the eternal spectres of the Alps rose before me in all their strength and calm. I was alone in the cabriolet, I do not know how to express what I felt. It seemed to me that these giants spoke to me of all the grandeurs that leave the hand of God. I am no more than a child, I cried to myself, but I have two great friends and they are happy. Write to me, my George. Be sure that I shall look after your affairs. May my friendship never be unfortunate to you. Respect it, this friendship more ardent than love, it is all that is good in me, think of that; it is the work of God. You are the thread that attaches me to Him; think of the life that awaits me.

FROM

George Sand

TO

Alfred Musset

Venice, May 1834

. . . I have here, near to me, my friend, my support, he does not suffer, he is not feeble, he is not suspicious, he has never known the bitternesses that used to corrode your heart; he has no need of my strength, he has his own calm and his own virtue. He loves me peacefully, he is happy without causing me suffering, without my having to work for his happiness. Ah, well, I need to suffer for someone, I need to employ my excess of energy and sensibility. I have need to use this sense of maternal solicitude that is used to watching over some weary, suffering creature Oh, why can I not live between you both and make you both happy, without belonging to either one or the other? I could have lived ten years like that . . . Alas, how the things of this world are vain and deceitful and how the heart of man changes when it hears the voice of God! I have listened for this, and I think that I have heard it. And yet men cry low words after me: Horror, madness, scandal, lies!—What does this mean? What is the cause of all these maledictions? Of what now am I accused:—I remember when I was in a convent, the rue Saint-Marceau passed behind our chapel. When the market women raised their voices one could hear their blasphemies even in the depth of the sanctuary. But for me it was merely a sound striking the outer walls that drew me from my prayers in the evening silence. I heard the noise, I understood nothing of the coarse oaths, I turned again to my devotions without either my ear or my heart being soiled by these blasphemies. Since, I have retired into love as into a sanctuary, and sometimes the foul abuse outside has made me raise my head, but it has not interrupted the hymn that I address to Heaven and I merely say to myself, these are the vulgar hucksters that pass by.

It is too late for me to go to Constantinople. The heat has come before my money arrived. I shall go another season, with Pagello, who hopes, perhaps with reason, to find some fortune out of such a journey. A steam boat service is being organised to take the passengers from Venice to Trieste through all the islands of the Archipelago. Be then, at peace for the present. I am still at Venice and I look after myself, for I am not absolutely well. I am always suffering, as you know—but you, how are you? I hope that you don't travel alone, and that you always keep Antonio with you. You still have him? You are pleased with him? He did not know what he meant to me when he left Venice—this hairdresser that took my place! Alas! Alas! Perhaps the most bitter and profound sigh of my life was in the sound of the wave that detached me from the bank of Fusina! Yes, we will return there in August, whatever happens, shall we not? You will then perhaps be engaged in another love-affair. I want that and yet I fear it. My child, I do not know what feelings are roused in me when I think of that possibility. If I could clasp her hand and tell her how you must be cherished and loved.

But she would be jealous. She will say to you—'Don't speak to me of Madame Sand, she is an infamous woman.' Ah, I, at least, can talk of you continually, without ever seeing a clouded brow, without hearing a bitter word. Your memory is like a sacred relic here, your name is a solemn word that I whisper sometimes in the evenings, across the silent lagoons, and that is answered by a faint voice, saying brief, sweet, simple words Io l'amo (I love you) that seem to me so beautiful! It does not matter, my child, love, be loved and may my memory never poison any of your joys. Sacrifice this memory, if you must. God be my witness, however, that I should despise anyone that suggested that I should not only curse you, but forget you.

Farewell, my little angel, if you rejoin God before I do, keep a little place up there for me, near to you—and be sure if I go first I shall keep a good one for you. Pagello charges me to say that he does not write to you for fear of troubling you, but that he embraces you with all his heart. As for me, I press you to my heart and bless you. I was about to write you another letter for the Revue. Tell me where I should address it, I want you to be the first to read it in manuscript. But if you are in Switzerland, so much travelling may destroy it. If you go to Aix, write to me from there and I will send it there: and you can send it direct to Buloz. Send me, with the other things that I asked for, some cigarette papers, my Beethoven symphonies, Weber's Valse Sentimentale and Vaccai's Juliette. You can bring the case with you and send it from Lyons or Geneva, so that it will cost me only half the carriage. Have you still our little birds?

Prince Albert

Queen Victoria

Victoria was sixteen years old when she met her prince. Her uncle had arranged the meeting between her and Albert, suggesting that the two should marry. Both were infatuated and deeply in love with each other, and were together for seventeen years. It was a happy marriage . . . on the surface.

Like all royal families, power struggles erupted in their relationship. Victoria's pregnancies proved to be an opportunity for Albert to take over most of her duties—a gesture first appreciated and then resented by the queen. She was fed up of being pregnant again and again; they had had nine children. Consequently, Victoria quite often lost her temper. Albert grew afraid that she might have inherited the madness of her grandfather, George III.

Despite of the problems in their marriage, they remained together till Albert's death. For the rest of her life, Victoria mourned her husband . . . but maybe not for long. She was suspected of having affairs with two of her servants, John Brown and Abdul Karim, after the king's passing.

15th November 1839

Dearest, deeply loved Victoria,

According to your wish, and by the urging of my heart to talk to you and open my heart to you, I send these lines. We arrived safely at Calais, and Lord Alfred Paget is to re-cross in a quarter of an hour, and will arrive at Windsor early tomorrow. The state of the tide and strong wind forced us to start at 2.30 in the morning, and we reached here at about 6 o'clock. Even then the Firebrand could not approach the quay, so that we decided to go ashore in a smaller boat. We both, Schenk, and all the servants were fearfully ill; I have hardly recovered yet. I need not tell you that since we left, all my thoughts have been with you at Windsor, and that your image fills my whole soul. Even in my dreams I never imagined that I should find so much love on earth. How that moment shines for me when I was close to you, but with your hand in mine! Those days flew by so quickly, but our separation will fly equally so. Ernest wishes me to say a thousand nice things to you. With promises of unchanging love and devotion, your ever true Albert.

My best respects to the aunt and Baroness Lehzen.

Nathaniel Hawthorne

Sophia Peabody

Sophia Peabody never intended to have a husband . . . or so she wrote in a letter to her sister in 1838, but little did she know that her future husband lived a block away from home. A year after writing this in a letter to her sister, she was secretly engaged to Nathaniel Hawthorne—a man who had arrived at the Peabody home to see Elizabeth but had ended up falling for her young sister.

Nathaniel and Sophia got married in 1842 and settled in Concord, Massachusetts. The Hawthornes kept private journals, and when Nathaniel and Sophia married, they started keeping a journal together. This was the first entry made by Nathaniel: A rainy day—a rainy day and I do verily believe there is no sunshine in this world, except what beams from my wife's eyes.

Brook Farm, Friday, July 9th, half past 5 p.m. (1841)

To Miss Peabody

Oh, unutterably ownest wife, no pen can write how I have longed for thee, or for any the slightest word from thee; for thy Sunday's letter did not reach me till noon of this very day! Never was such a thirst of the spirit as I have felt. I began to wonder whether my Dove did really exist, or was only a vision; and canst thou imagine what a desolate feeling that was. Oh, I need thee, my wife, every day, and every hour, and every minute, and every minutest particle of forever and forever.

Belovedest, the robe reached me in due season, and on Sabbath day, I put it on; and truly it imparted such a noble and stately aspect to thy husband, that thou couldst not possibly have known him. He did really look tolerably personable! and, moreover, he felt as if thou wert embracing him, all the time that he was wrapt in the folds of this precious robe. Hast thou made it of such immortal stuff as the robes of Bunyan's Pilgrim were made of? else it would grieve my very heart to subject it to the wear and tear of the world.

Belovedest, when dost thou mean to come home? It is a whole eternity since I saw thee. If thou art at home on a Sunday, I must and will spend it with my ownest wife. Oh, how my heart leaps at the thought.

God bless thee, thou belovedest woman-angel! I cannot write a single word more; for I have stolen the time to write this from the labors of the field. I ought to be raking hay, like my brethren, who will have to labor the longer and later, on account of these few moments which I have given to thee. Now that we are in the midst of haying, we return to our toil, after an early supper. I think I never felt so vigorous as now; but, oh, I cannot be well without thee. Farewell,

Thine Ownest.

❦

Brook Farm, October 21st, 1841—Noon

Ownest beloved, I know thou dost not care in the least about receiving a word from thy husband—thou lovest me not—in fact thou hast quite forgotten that such a person exists. I do love thee so much, that I really think that all the love is on my side;—there is no room for any more in the whole universe.

Sweetest, I have nothing at all to say to thee—nothing, I mean, that regards this external world;

and as to matters of the heart and soul, they are not to be written about. What atrocious weather! In all this month, we have not had a single truly October day; it has been a real November month, and of the most disagreeable kind. I came to this place in one snowstorm, and shall probably leave it in another; so that my reminiscences of Brook Farm are like to be the coldest and dreariest imaginable. But next month, thou, belovedest, will be my sunshine and my summer. No matter what weather it may be then.

Dearest, good bye. Dost thou love me after all? Art thou magnificently well? God bless thee. Thou didst make me infinitely happiest, at our last meeting. Was it a pleasant season likewise to thee?

Thine ownest,
Theodore de L'Aubepine.

Miss Sophia A. Peabody,
Care of Dr. N. Peabody,
Boston, Mass.

Daniel Webster

Josephine Seaton

The orator and statesman Daniel Webster penned the following letter to a woman who had forgotten her bonnet at his house.

March 1844

My Dear Josephine,

I fear you got a wetting last evening, as it rained fast soon after you left our door; and I avail myself of the return of your bonnet, to express the wish that you are well this morning, and without cold.

I have demanded parlance with your Bonnet: have asked it how many tender looks it has noticed to be directed under it; what soft words it has heard, close to its side; in what instances an air of triumph has caused it to be tossed; and whether, ever, and when, it has quivered from trembling emotions, proceeding from below. But it has proved itself a faithful keeper of secrets, and would answer none of my questions. It only remained for me to attempt to surprise it into confession, by pronouncing sundry names, one after another. It seemed quite unmoved by most of these, but at the apparently unexpected mention of one, I thought its ribands decidedly fluttered!

I gave it my parting good wishes; hoping that it might never cover an aching head, and that the eyes which it protects from the rays of the sun, may know no tears but those of joy and affection.

Yours, dear Josephine, with affectionate regard.

Danl. Webster

Robert Browning

Elizabeth Barrett

In 1842, Robert Browning had published his collection of poems, Dramatic Lyrics, *in which he had penned poetry in the style of a dramatic monologue. Many of the readers had criticized this style . . . many except Elizabeth Barrett. Browning then wrote to thank her for praising his work, asking her to meet him. They met, and they fell in love. All was good, until Barrett's father expressed his dissatisfaction.*

Barrett eloped with Browning in 1846. She came back home a week later, keeping her marriage a secret, and then left for Italy. The couple had a happy marriage and spent a blissful fifteen years with each other, until Barrett's death in 1861. She died in her husband's arms.

New Cross, Hatcham, Surrey.

January 10, 1845

I love your verses with all my heart, dear Miss
Barrett,—and this is no off-hand complimentary
letter that I shall write,—whatever else, no prompt
matter-of-course recognition of your genius, and
there a graceful and natural end of the thing. Since
the day last week when I first read your poems, I
quite laugh to remember how I have been turning
and turning again in my mind what I should be
able to tell you of their effect upon me, for in the
first flush of delight I thought I would this once
get out of my habit of purely passive enjoyment,
when I do really enjoy, and thoroughly justify
my admiration—perhaps even, as a loyal fellow-
craftsman should, try and find fault and do you
some little good to be proud of hereafter!—but
nothing comes of it all—so into me has it gone,
and part of me has it become, this great living
poetry of yours, not a flower of which but took
root and grew—Oh, how different that is from
lying to be dried and pressed flat, and prized highly,
and put in a book with a proper account at top and
bottom, and shut up and put away . . . and the book
called a 'Flora,' besides! After all, I need not give

up the thought of doing that, too, in time; because even now, talking with whoever is worthy, I can give a reason for my faith in one and another excellence, the fresh strange music, the affluent language, the exquisite pathos and true new brave thought; but in this addressing myself to you—your own self, and for the first time, my feeling rises altogether. I do, as I say, love these books with all my heart—and I love you too. Do you know I was once not very far from seeing—really seeing you? Mr. Kenyon said to me one morning 'Would you like to see Miss Barrett?' then he went to announce me,—then he returned . . . you were too unwell, and now it is years ago, and I feel as at some untoward passage in my travels, as if I had been close, so close, to some world's-wonder in chapel or crypt, only a screen to push and I might have entered, but there was some slight, so it now seems, slight and just sufficient bar to admission, and the half-opened door shut, and I went home my thousands of miles, and the sight was never to be?

Well, these Poems were to be, and this true thankful joy and pride with which I feel myself,

Yours ever faithfully,
Robert Browning.

Miss Barrett, 1
50 Wimpole St.
R. Browning.

❧

Monday Morning.

Post-mark, December 15, 1845

Every word you write goes to my heart and lives there: let us live so, and die so, if God will. I trust many years hence to begin telling you what I feel now;—that the beam of the light will have reached you!—meantime it is here. Let me kiss your forehead, my sweetest, dearest.

Wednesday I am waiting for—how waiting for!

After all, it seems probable that there was no intentional mischief in that jeweller's management of the ring. The divided gold must have been exposed to fire—heated thoroughly, perhaps,—and what became of the contents then! Well, all is safe now, and I go to work again of course. My next act is just done—that is, being done—but, what I did not foresee, I cannot bring it, copied, by Wednesday, as my sister went this morning on a visit for the week.

On the matters, the others, I will not think, as you bid me,—if I can help, at least. But your kind, gentle, good sisters! and the provoking sorrow of the right meaning at bottom of the wrong doing—wrong to itself and its plain purpose—and meanwhile, the real tragedy and sacrifice of a life!

If you should see Mr. Kenyon, and can find if he will be disengaged on Wednesday evening, I shall be glad to go in that case.

But I have been writing, as I say, and will leave off this, for the better communing with you. Don't imagine I am unwell; I feel quite well, but a little tired, and the thought of you waits in such readiness! So, may God bless you, beloved!

I am all your own

R.B.

෧෨෬

1 p.m. Saturday

Post-mark, September 12, 1846

You will only expect a few words—what will those be? When the heart is full it may run over, but the real fulness stays within.

You asked me yesterday 'if I should repent?' Yes—my own Ba,—I could wish all the past were to do over again, that in it I might somewhat more,—never so little more, conform in the outward homage to the inward feeling. What I have professed ... (for I have performed nothing) seems to fall short of what my first love required even—and when I think of this moment's love ... I could repent, as I say.

Words can never tell you, however,—form them, transform them anyway,—how perfectly dear you are to me—perfectly dear to my heart and soul.

I look back, and in every one point, every word and gesture, every letter, every silence—you have been entirely perfect to me—I would not change one word, one look.

My hope and aim are to preserve this love, not to fall from it—for which I trust to God who procured it for me, and doubtlessly can preserve it.

Enough now, my dearest, dearest, own Ba! You have given me the highest, completest proof of love that ever one human being gave another. I am all gratitude—and all pride (under the proper feeling which ascribes pride to the right source) all pride that my life has been so crowned by you.

God bless you prays your very own

R.

I will write tomorrow of course. Take every care of my life which is in that dearest little hand; try and be composed, my beloved.

Remember to thank Wilson for me.

Elizabeth Barrett

Robert Browning

Saturday, January 1845

I thank you, dear Mr. Browning, from the bottom of my heart. You meant to give me pleasure by your letter—and even if the object had not been answered, I ought still to thank you. But it is thoroughly answered. Such a letter from such a hand! Sympathy is dear—very dear to me: but the sympathy of a poet, and of such a poet, is the quintessence of sympathy to me! Will you take back my gratitude for it?—agreeing, too, that of all the commerce done in the world, from Tyre to Carthage, the exchange of sympathy for gratitude is the most princely thing!

For the rest you draw me on with your

kindness. It is difficult to get rid of people when you once have given them too much pleasure—that is a fact, and we will not stop for the moral of it. What I was going to say—after a little natural hesitation—is, that if ever you emerge without inconvenient effort from your 'passive state', and will tell me of such faults as rise to the surface and strike you as important in my poems, (for of course, I do not think of troubling you with criticism in detail) you will confer a lasting obligation on me, and one which I shall value so much, that I covet it at a distance. I do not pretend to any extraordinary meekness under criticism and it is possible enough that I might not be altogether obedient to yours. But with my high respect for your power in your Art and for your experience as an artist, it would be quite impossible for me to hear a general observation of yours on what appear to you my master-faults, without being the better for it hereafter in some way. I ask for only a sentence or two of general observation—and I do not ask even for that, so as to tease you—but in the humble, low voice, which is so excellent a thing in women—particularly when they go a-begging! The most frequent general criticism I receive, is, I think, upon the style,—'if I would but change my style'! But that is an objection (isn't it?) to the writer bodily? Buffon says, and every sincere writer must feel, that 'Le style c'est l'homme'; a fact, however, scarcely calculated to lessen the objection with certain critics.

Is it indeed true that I was so near to the pleasure and honour of making your acquaintance? and can it be true that you look back upon the lost opportunity with any regret? But—you know—if you had entered the 'crypt,' you might have caught cold, or been tired to death, and wished yourself 'a thousand miles off;' which would have been worse than travelling them. It is not my interest, however, to put such thoughts in your head about its being 'all for the best'; and I would rather hope (as I do) that what I lost by one chance I may recover by some future one. Winters shut me up as they do dormouse's eyes; in the spring, we shall see: and I am so much better that I seem turning round to the outward world again. And in the meantime I have learnt to know your voice, not merely from the poetry but from the kindness in it. Mr. Kenyon often speaks of you—dear Mr. Kenyon!—who most unspeakably, or only speakably with tears in my eyes,—has been my friend and helper, and my book's friend and helper! critic and sympathiser, true friend of all hours! You know him well enough, I think, to understand that I must be grateful to him.

I am writing too much,—and notwithstanding that I am writing too much, I will write of one thing more. I will say that I am your debtor, not only for this cordial letter and for all the pleasure which came with it, but in other ways, and those the highest: and I will say that while I live to follow this divine art of poetry, in proportion to my love for it and my devotion to it, I must be a devout admirer and student of your works. This is in my heart to say to you—and I say it.

And, for the rest, I am proud to remain

Your obliged and faithful
Elizabeth B. Barrett.

Robert Browning, Esq.
New Cross, Hatcham, Surrey.

Thursday Morning.

Post-mark, April 18, 1845

If you did but know dear Mr. Browning how often I have written . . . not this letter I am about to write, but another better letter to you, . . . in the midst of my silence, . . . you would not think for a moment that the east wind, with all the harm it does to me, is able to do the great harm of putting out the light of the thought of you to my mind; for this, indeed, it has no power to do. I had the pen in my hand once to write; and why it fell out, I cannot tell you. And you see, . . . all your writing will not change the wind! You wished all manner of good to me one day as the clock struck ten; yes, and I assure you I was better that day—and I must not forget to tell you so though it is so long since. And therefore, I was logically bound to believe that you had never thought of me since . . . unless you thought east winds of me! That was quite clear; was it not? or would have been; if it had not been for the supernatural conviction, I had above all, of your kindness, which was too large to be taken in the hinge of a syllogism. In fact I have long left off thinking that logic proves anything—it doesn't, you know.

But your Lamia has taught you some subtle 'viperine' reasoning and motiving, for the turning down one street instead of another. It was conclusive.

Ah—but you will never persuade me that I am the better, or as well, for the thing that I have not. We look from different points of view, and yours is the point of attainment. Not that you do not truly say that, when all is done, we must come home to place our engines, and act by our own strength. I do not want material as material; no one does—but every life requires a full experience, a various experience—and I have a profound conviction that where a poet has been shut from most of the outward aspects of life, he is at a lamentable disadvantage. Can you, speaking for yourself, separate the results in you from the external influences at work around you, that you say so boldly that you get nothing from the world? You do not directly, I know—but you do indirectly and by a rebound. Whatever acts upon you, becomes you—and whatever you love or hate, whatever charms you or is scorned by you, acts on you and becomes you. Have you read the 'Improvisatore'? or will you? The writer seems to feel, just as I do, the good of the outward life; and he is a poet in his soul. It is a book full of beauty and had a great charm to me.

As to the Polkas and Cellariuses I do not covet them of course . . . but what a strange world you seem to have, to me at a distance—what a strange husk of a world! How it looks to me like mandarin-life or something as remote; nay, not mandarin-life but mandarin manners, . . . life, even the outer life, meaning something deeper, in my account of it. As to dear Mr. Kenyon I do not make the mistake of fancying that many can look like him or talk like him or be like him. I know enough to know otherwise. When he spoke of me he should have said that I was better notwithstanding the east wind. It is really true—I am getting slowly up from the prostration of the severe cold, and feel stronger in myself.

But Mrs. Norton discourses excellent music—and for the rest, there are fruits in the world so over-ripe, that they will fall, . . . without being gathered. Let Maynooth witness to it! if you think it worth while!

Ever yours,

Elizabeth B. Barrett.

And is it nothing to be 'justified to one's self in one's resources?' 'That's all,' indeed! For the 'soul's country' we will have it also—and I know how well the birds sing in it. How glad I was by the way to see your letter!

Sunday, September 14, 1846

My own beloved, if ever you should have reason to complain of me in things voluntary and possible, all other women would have a right to tread me underfoot, I should be so vile and utterly unworthy. There is my answer to what you wrote yesterday of wishing to be better to me . . . you! What could be better than lifting me from the ground and carrying me into life and the sunshine? I was yours rather by right than by gift (yet by gift also, my beloved!); for what you have saved and renewed is surely yours. All that I am, I owe you—if I enjoy anything now and henceforth, it is through you. You know this well. Even as I, from the beginning, knew that I had no power against you . . . or that, if I had it was for your sake.

Dearest, in the emotion and confusion of yesterday morning, there was yet room in me for one thought which was not a feeling—for I thought that, of the many, many women who have stood where I stood, and to the same end, not one of them all perhaps, not one perhaps, since that building was a church, has had reasons strong as mine, for an absolute trust and devotion towards the man she married,—not one! And then I both thought and felt, that it was only just, for them . . . those women who were less happy, . . . to have that affectionate sympathy and support and presence of their nearest relations, parent or sister . . . which failed to me, . . . needing it less through being happier!

All my brothers have been here this morning, laughing and talking, and discussing this matter of the leaving town,—and in the room, at the same time, were two or three female friends of ours, from Herefordshire—and I did not dare to cry out against the noise, though my head seemed splitting in two (one-half for each shoulder), I had such a morbid fear of exciting a suspicion. Treppy too being one of them, I promised to go to see her tomorrow and dine in her drawing room if she would give me, for dinner, some bread and butter. It was like having a sort of fever. And all in the midst, the bells began to ring. "What bells are those?" asked one of the provincials. "Marylebone Church bells," said Henrietta, standing behind my chair.

And now . . . while I write, having escaped from the great din, and sit here quietly,—comes . . . who do you think?—Mr. Kenyon.

He came with his spectacles, looking as if his eyes reached to their rim all the way round; and one of the first words was, "When did you see Browning?" And I think I shall make a pretension to presence of mind henceforward; for, though certainly I changed colour and he saw it, I yet answered with a tolerably quick evasion . . . He was here on Friday—and leapt straight into another subject, and left him gazing fixedly on my face. Dearest, he saw something, but not all. So we talked, talked. He told me that the 'Fawn of Sertorius' (which I refused to cut open the other day) was ascribed to Landor and he told me that he meant to leave town again on Wednesday, and would see me once before then. On rising to go away, he mentioned your name a second time . . . "When do you see Browning again?" To which I answered that I did not know.

Is not that pleasant? The worst is that all these combinations of things make me feel so bewildered that I cannot make the necessary arrangements, as far as the letters go. But I must break from the dream-stupor which falls on me when left to myself a little, and set about what remains to be done.

A house near Watford is thought of now—but, as none is concluded on, the removal is not likely to take place in the middle of the week even, perhaps.

I sit in a dream, when left to myself. I cannot believe, or understand. Oh! but in all this difficult, embarrassing and painful situation, I look over the palms to Troy—I feel happy and exulting to belong to you, past every opposition, out of sight of every will of man—none can put us asunder, now, at least.

I have a right now openly to love you, and to hear other people call it a duty, when I do, . . . knowing that if it were a sin, it would be done equally. Ah—I shall not be first to leave off that—see if I shall! May God bless you, ever and ever dearest! Beseech for me the indulgence of your father and mother, and ask your sister to love me. I feel so as if I had slipped down over the wall into somebody's garden—I feel ashamed. To be grateful and affectionate to them all, while I live, is all that I can do, and it is too much a matter of course to need to be promised. Promise it however for your very own Ba whom you made so happy with the dear letter last night.

But say in the next how you are—and how your mother is.

I did hate so, to have to take off the ring! You will have to take the trouble of putting it on again, some day.

John Ruskin

Effie Gray

John and Effie had known each other since they were children. The Grays had even moved into the Ruskin house after Effie's father had shifted to London for business. Head over heels in love, John proposed but was rejected.

At the time, Effie was eyeing other young, handsome men. Perhaps her father had been the one to make her realize that marriage into the wealthy Ruskin family could save their own financial troubles. The marriage didn't last long. After six years, Effie got the marriage annulled for non-consummation. The reason behind this is still debated, though the popular opinion is that Ruskin had found out that Effie had married him for his money. After this, he had lost all his love for her.

30 November 1847

My Beloved Effie,

I never thought to have felt time pass slowly any more—but—foolish that I am, I cannot help congratulating myself on this being the last day of November—Foolish, I say—for what pleasure soever may be in store for us, we ought not to wish to lose the treasure of time—nor to squander away the heap of gold even though its height should keep us from seeing each other for a little while. But your letter of last night shook all the philosopher out of me. That little undress bit! Ah my sweet Lady—What naughty thoughts had I. Dare I say?—I was thinking—thinking, naughty—happy thought, that you would soon have—someone's arms to keep you from being cold! Pray don't be angry with me. How could I help it?—how can I? I'm thinking so just now, even. Oh—my dearest—I am not so scornful' neither, of all that I hope for.—Alas—I know not what I would not give for one glance of your fair eyes—your fair—saucy eyes. You cruel, cruel girl—now that was just like you—to poor William at the Ball. I can see you at this moment—hear you. 'If you wanted to dance with me, William! If!' You saucy—wicked—witching—malicious—merciless—

mischief-loving—torturing—martyrizing—unspeakably to be feared and fled—mountain nymph that you are—'If!' When you knew that he would have given a year of is life for a touch of your hand. Ah's me—what a world this is, when its best creatures and kindest—will do such things. What a sad world. Poor fellow,—How the lights of the ball room would darken and its floor ink beneath him—Earthquake and eclipse at once, and to be 'if'd' at by you, too; Now—I'll take up his injured cause—I'll punish you for that—Effie—some time—see if I don't—If I don't. It deserves—oh—I don't know what it doesn't deserve—now what I can do.

P.S. Ah—my mysterious girl—I forgot one little bit of the letter—but I can't forget all, though 'a great many things'.

My heart is yours—my thoughts—myself—all but my memory, but that's mine. Now it is cool—as you say—to give me all that pain—and then tell me—'Never mind, I won't do it again.' Heaven forbid! How could you—puss? You are not thinking of saying that you have 'been thinking about it—' or 'writing to a friend'—and that you won't have me now! Are you?

Edgar Allan Poe

Sarah Helen Whitman

It was 1845. Edgar Allan Poe was walking with his friend, Frances Sergeant Osgood. They passed by a house with a beautiful garden. A lady was standing behind one of the rose bushes. Osgood knew her and asked Poe if he wanted to be introduced to her. Poe declined.

This woman was Sarah Helen Whitman, a wealthy widow who lived in Rhode Island, Providence. She met Poe on 21 September 1848, and they fell in love. After a brief but feverish courtship, Sarah agreed to marry him, but her mother was against it. The engagement was broken, and they never saw each other again.

Sunday Night

October 1, 1848

I have pressed your letter again and again to my
lips, sweetest Helen—bathing it in tears of joy, or
of a 'divine despair'. But I—who so lately, in your
presence, vaunted the 'power of words'—of what
avail are mere words to me now? Could I believe
in the efficiency of prayers to the God of Heaven,
I would indeed kneel—humbly kneel—at this the
most earnest epoch of my life—kneel in entreaty
for words—but for words that should disclose to
you—that might enable me to lay bare to you my
whole heart. All thoughts—all passions seem now
merged in that one consuming desire—the mere
wish to make you comprehend—to make you
see that for which there is no human voice—the
unutterable fervor of my love for you:—for so well
do I know your poet-nature, oh Helen, Helen! that
I feel sure if you could but look down now into
the depths of my soul with your pure spiritual eyes
you could not refuse to speak to me what, alas! you
still resolutely have unspoken—you would love
me if only for the greatness of my love. Is it not
something in this cold, dreary world, to be loved?—
Oh, if I could but burn into your spirit the deep—

the true meaning which I attach to those three syllables underlined!—but, alas: the effort is all in vain and I live and die unheard.

When I spoke to you of what I felt, saying that I loved now for the first time, I did not hope you would believe or even understand me; nor can I hope to convince you now—but if, throughout some long, dark summer night, I could but have held you close, close to my heart and whispered to you the strange secrets of its passionate history, then indeed you would have seen that I have been far from attempting to deceive you in this respect. I could have shown you that it was not and could never have been in the power of any other than yourself to move me as I am now moved—to oppress me with this ineffable emotion—to surround and bathe me in this electric light, illumining and enkindling my whole nature—filling my soul with glory, with wonder, and with awe. During our walk in the cemetery I said to you, while the bitter, bitter tears sprang into my eyes—"Helen, I love now—now—for the first and only time." I said this, I repeat, in no hope that you could believe me, but because I could not help feeling how unequal were the heart-riches we might offer each to each:—I, for the first time, giving my all at once, and forever, even while the words of your poem were yet ringing in my ears:—

Oh then, beloved, I think on thee
And on that life so strangely fair
Ere yet one cloud of Memory
Had gathered in Hope's golden air.
I think on thee and thy lone grave
On the green hill-side far away—
I see the wilding flowers that wave
Around thee as the night-winds sway;
And still, though only clouds remain
On Life's horizon, cold and drear,
The dream of Youth returns again
With the sweet promise of the year.

Ah Helen, these lines are indeed beautiful, beautiful—but their very beauty was cruelty to me. Why—why did you show them to me? There seemed, too, so very especial a purpose in what you did.

I have already told you that some few casual words spoken of you—not very kindly—by Miss Lynch, were the first in which I had ever heard your name mentioned. She described you, in some measure, personally. She alluded to what she called your 'eccentricities' and hinted at your sorrows. Her description of the former strangely arrested—her half sneers at the latter enchained and riveted, my attention. She had referred to thoughts, sentiments, traits, moods which I knew to be my own, but which, until that moment, I had believed to be my own solely—unshared by any human being. A profound sympathy took immediate possession of my soul. I cannot better explain to you what I felt than by saying that your unknown heart seemed to pass into my bosom—there to dwell forever—while mine, I thought, was translated into your own. From that hour I loved you. Yes, I now feel that it was then—on that evening of sweet dreams—that the very first dawn of human love burst upon the icy Night of my spirit. Since that period I have never seen nor heard your name without a shiver half of delight, half of anxiety. The impression left, however, upon my mind, by Miss Lynch (whether through my own fault or her design I know not) was that you were a wife now and a most happy one;—and it is only within the last few months that I have been undeceived in this respect. For this reason I shunned your presence and even the city in which you lived.—You may remember that once, when I passed through Providence with Mrs. Osgood, I positively refused to accompany her to your house, and even provoked her into a quarrel by the obstinacy and seeming unreasonableness of my refusal. I fared neither go nor say why I could not. I fared not speak of you—much less see you. For years your name never passed my lips, while my soul drank in, with a delirious thirst, all that was uttered in my presence respecting you. The merest whisper that concerned you awoke in me a shuddering sixth sense, vaguely compounded of fear, ecstatic happiness, and a wild, inexplicable sentiment that resembled nothing so nearly as the consciousness of guilt.——Judge, then, with what wondering, unbelieving joy I received in your well-known MS., the Valentine which first gave me to see that you knew me to exist. The idea of what men call Fate lost then for the first time, in my eyes, its character of futility. I felt that nothing hereafter was to be doubted, and lost myself, for many weeks, in one continuous, delicious dream, where all was a vivid yet indistinct bliss.——Immediately after reading the Valentine, I wished to contrive some mode of acknowledging——without wounding you by seeming directly to acknowledge——my sense——oh, my keen——my profound——my exulting——my ecstatic sense of the honor you had conferred on me. To accomplish, as I wished it, precisely what I wished, seemed impossible, however; and I was on the point of abandoning the idea, when my eyes fell upon a volume of my own poems; and then the lines I had written, in my passionate boyhood, to the first, purely ideal love of my soul——to the Helen Stannard of whom I told you——flashed upon my recollection. I turned to them. They expressed all——all that I would have said to you—so fully—so accurately and so exclusively, that a thrill of intense superstition ran at once throughout my frame. Read the verses and then take into consideration the peculiar need I had, at the moment, for just so seemingly unattainable a mode of communicating with you as they afforded. Think of the absolute appositeness with which they fulfilled that need—expressing not only all that I would have said of your person, but all that of which I most wished to assure you, in the lines commencing 'On desperate seas long wont to roam.' Think, too, of the rare agreement of name—Helen and not the far more usual Ellen—think of all these coincidences, and you will no longer wonder that, to one accustomed as I am to the Calculus of Probabilities, they wore an air of positive miracle. There was but one difficulty.—I did not wish to copy the lines in my own MS—nor did I wish you to trace them to my volume of poems. I hoped to leave at least something of doubt on your mind as to how, why, and especially whence they came. And now, when, on accidentally turning the leaf, I found even this difficulty obviated, by the poem happening to be the last in the book, thus having no letter-press on its reverse—I yielded at once to an overwhelming sense of Fatality. From that hour I have never been able to shake from my soul the belief that my Destiny, for good or for evil, either here or hereafter, is in some measure interwoven with your own.—Of course, I did not expect on your part any acknowledgment of the printed lines 'To Helen'; and yet, without confessing it even to myself, I experienced an undefinable sorrow in your silence. At length, when I thought you had time fully to forget me (if indeed you had ever really remembered) I sent you the anonymous lines in MS. I wrote them, first, through a pining, burning desire to communicate with you in some way—even if you remained in ignorance of your correspondent. The mere thought that your dear fingers would press—your sweet eyes dwell upon characters which I had penned—characters which had welled out upon the paper from the depths of so devout a love—filled my soul with a rapture which seemed then all sufficient for my human nature. It then appeared to me that merely this one thought involved so much of bliss that here on Earth I could have no right ever to repine—no room for discontent.—If ever, then, I dared to picture for myself a richer happiness, it was always connected with your image in Heaven. But there was yet another idea which impelled me to send you those lines:—I said to myself—The sentiment—the holy passion which glows within my spirit for her, is of Heaven, heavenly, and has no taint of the Earth.

Thus there must lie, in the recesses of her own pure bosom, at least the germ of a reciprocal love; and if this be indeed so, she will need no earthly clew—she will indistinctly feel who is her correspondent.—In this case, then, I may hope for some faint token, at least, giving me to understand that the source of the poem is known and its sentiment comprehended even if disapproved. Oh God! how long—how long I waited in vain—hoping against Hope—until at length I became possessed with a spirit far sterner—far more reckless than Despair.—I explained to you—but without detailing the vital influence they wrought upon my fortune—those singular additional yet seemingly trivial fatalities by which you happened to address your lines to Fordham in place of New York—by which my aunt happened to get notice of their being in the West-Farms Post Office—and by which it happened that, of all my set of the 'Home Journal', I failed in receiving only that individual number which contained your published verses; but I have not yet told you that your MS. lines reached me in Richmond on the very day in which I was about to depart on a tour and an enterprize which would have changed my very nature—fearfully altered my very soul—steeped me in a stern, cold and debasing, although brilliant and gigantic ambition—and borne me 'far, far away' and forever, from you, sweet, sweet Helen, and from this divine dream of your Love.

And now, in the most simple words at my command, let me paint to you the impression made upon me by your personal presence.—As you entered the room, pale, timid, hesitating, and evidently oppressed at heart; as your eyes rested appealingly, for one brief moment, upon mine, I felt, for the first time in my life, and tremblingly acknowledged, the existence of spiritual influences altogether out of the reach of the reason. I saw that you were Helen—my Helen—the Helen of a thousand dreams—she whose visionary lips had so often lingered upon my own in the divine trance of passion—she whom the great Giver of all Good had preordained to be mine—mine only—if not now, alas! then at least hereafter and forever, in the Heavens.—You spoke falteringly and seemed scarcely conscious of what you said. I heard no words—only the soft voice, more familiar to me than my own, and more melodious than the songs of the angels. Your hand rested within mine, and my whole soul shook with a tremulous ecstasy. And then but for very shame—but for the fear of grieving or oppressing you—I would have fallen at your feet in as pure—in as real a worship as was ever offered to Idol or to God. And when, afterwards, on those two successive evenings of all-heavenly delight, you passed to and fro about the room—now sitting by my side, now far away, now standing with your hand resting on the back of my chair, while the praeternatural thrill of your touch vibrated even through the senseless wood into my heart—while you moved thus restlessly about the room—as if a deep Sorrow or a more profound Joy haunted your bosom—my brain reeled beneath the intoxicating spell of your presence, and it was with no merely human senses that I either saw or heard you. It was my soul only that distinguished you there. I grew faint with the luxury of your voice and blind with the voluptuous lustre of your eyes.

Let me quote to you a passage from your letter:—"You will, perhaps, attempt to convince me that my person is agreeable to you—that my countenance interests you:—but in this respect I am so variable that I should inevitably disappoint you if you hoped to find in me tomorrow the same aspect which won you today. And, again, although my reverence for your intellect and my admiration of your genius make me feel like a child in your presence, you are not, perhaps, aware that I am many years older than yourself. I fear you do not know it, and that if you had known it you would not have felt for me as you do."—To all this what shall I—what can I say—except that the heavenly candor with which you speak oppresses my heart with so rich a burden of love that my eyes overflow with sweet tears. You are mistaken, Helen, very far mistaken about this matter of age. I am older than you; and if illness and sorrow have made you seem older than you are—is not all this the best of reason for my loving you the more? Cannot my patient cares— my watchful, earnest attention—cannot the magic which lies in such devotion as I feel for you, win back for you much—oh, very much of the freshness of your youth? But grant that what you urge were even true. Do you not feel in your inmost heart of hearts that the 'soul-love' of which the world speaks so often and so idly is, in this instance at least, but the veriest, the most absolute of realities? Do you not—I ask it of your reason, darling, not less than of your heart—do you not perceive that it is my diviner nature—my spiritual being—which burns and pants to commingle with your own? Has the soul age, Helen? Can Immortality regard Time? Can that which began never and shall never end, consider a few wretched years of its incarnate life? Ah, I could weep—I could almost be angry with you for the unwarranted wrong you offer to the purity—to the sacred reality of my affection.—And how am I to answer what you say of your personal appearance?

Have I not seen you, Helen, have I not heard the more than melody of your voice? Has not my heart ceased to throb beneath the magic of your smile? Have I not held your hand in mine and looked steadily into your soul through the crystal Heaven of your eyes? Have I not done all these things?—or do I dream?—or am I mad? Were you indeed all that your fancy, enfeebled and perverted by illness, tempts you to suppose that you are, still, life of my life! I would but love you—but worship you the more:—it would be so glorious a happiness to be able to prove to you what I feel! But as it is, what can I—what am I to say? Who ever spoke of you without emotion— without praise? Who ever saw you and did not love?

But now a deadly terror oppresses me; for I too clearly see that these objections—so groundless— so futile when urged to one whose nature must be so well known to you as mine is—can scarcely be meant earnestly; and I tremble lest they but serve to mask others, more real, and which you hesitate—perhaps in pity—to confide to me. Alas! I too distinctly perceive, also, that in no instance you have ever permitted yourself to say that you love me. You are aware, sweet Helen, that on my part there are insuperable reasons forbidding me to urge upon you my love. Were I not poor—had not my late errors and reckless excesses justly lowered me in the esteem of the good—were I wealthy, or could I offer you worldly honors—ah then—then—how proud would I be to persevere—to sue—to plead—to kneel—to pray—to beseech you for your love—in the deepest humility—at your feet—at your feet, Helen, and with floods of passionate tears.

And now let me copy here one other passage from your letter:—"I find that I cannot now tell you all that I promised. I can only say to you [that had I youth and health and beauty, I would live for you and die with you. Now, were I to allow myself to love you, I could only enjoy a bright, brief hour of rapture and die . . . may God forever shield you from the agony which these your words occasion me! How selfish—how despicably selfish seems now all—all that I have written! Have I not, indeed, been demanding at your hands a love which might endanger your life? You will never, never know—you can never picture to yourself the hopeless, rayless despair with which I now trace these words. Alas Helen! my soul!—what is it that I have been saying to you?—to what madness have I been urging you?—I who am nothing to you—you who have a dear mother and sister to be blessed by your life and love. But ah, darling! if I seem selfish, yet believe that I truly, truly love you, and that it is the most spiritual of love that I speak, even if I speak it from the

depths of the most passionate of hearts. Think—
oh, think for me, Helen, and for yourself! Is there no
hope?—is there none? May not this terrible disease
be conquered? Frequently it has been overcome.
And more frequently are we deceived in respect to its
actual existence. Long-continued nervous disorder—
especially when exasperated by ether or excision—
will give rise to all the symptoms of heart-disease and
so deceive the most skillful physicians—as even in
my own case they were deceived. But admit that this
fearful evil has indeed assailed you. Do you not all
the more really need the devotionate care which only
one who loves you as I do, could or would bestow?
On my bosom could I not still the throbbings of
your own? Do not mistake me, Helen! Look, with
your searching—your seraphic eyes, into the soul of
my soul, and see if you can discover there one taint
of an ignoble nature! At your feet—if you so willed
it—I would cast from me, forever, all merely human
desire, and clothe myself in the glory of a pure, calm,
and unexacting affection. I would comfort you—
soothe you—tranquillize you. My love—my faith—
should instil into your bosom a praeternatural calm.
You would rest from care—from all worldly agitation.
You would get better, and finally well. And if not,
Helen,—if not—if you died—then at least would
I clasp your dear hand in death, and willingly—oh,

joyfully—joyfully—joyfully—go down with you into the night of the Grave.

Write soon—soon—oh, soon!—but not much. Do not weary or agitate yourself for my sake. Say to me those coveted words which would turn Earth into Heaven. If Hope is forbidden, I will not murmur if you comfort me with Love.— The papers of which you speak I will procure and forward immediately. They will cost me nothing, fear Helen, and I therefore re-enclose you what you so thoughtfully sent. Think that, in doing so, my lips are pressed fervently and lingeringly upon your own. And now, in closing this long, long letter, let me speak last of that which lies nearest my heart— of that precious gift which I would not exchange for the surest hope of Paradise. It seems to me too sacred that I should even whisper to you, the dear giver, what it is. My soul, this night, shall come to you in dreams and speak to you those fervid thanks which my pen is all powerless to utter.

Edgar

P. S. Tuesday Morning.—I beg you to believe, dear Helen, that I replied to your letter immediately upon its receipt; but a most unusual storm, up to this moment, precludes all access to the City.

FROM
Emily Dickinson
TO
Susan Gilbert

Emily Dickinson and Susan Gilbert first met each other at Amherst Academy. They started exchanging letters in their teens, and in the hundreds of letters that they wrote to each other, some showcase the warm affection Dickinson had for her friend, while some others are full of passion and playfulness.

These beautiful and heart-warming letters dwindled when Susan Gilbert married Emily Dickinson's brother, Austin.

11 June 1852

I have but one thought, Susie, this afternoon of June, and that of you, and I have one prayer, only; dear Susie, that is for you. That you and I in hand as we e'en do in heart, might ramble away as children, among the woods and fields, and forget these many years, and these sorrowing cares, and each become a child again—I would it were so, Susie, and when I look around me and find myself alone, I sigh for you again; little sigh, and vain sigh, which will not bring you home.

I need you more and more, and the great world grows wider, and dear ones fewer and fewer, every day that you stay away—I miss my biggest heart; my own goes wandering round, and calls for Susie—Friends are too dear to sunder, Oh they are far too few, and how soon they will go away where you and I cannot find them, dont let us forget these things, for their remembrance now will save us many an anguish when it is too late to love them! Susie, forgive me Darling, for every word I say—my heart is full of you, none other than you in my thoughts, yet when I seek to say to you something not for the world, words fail me. If you were here—and Oh that you were, my Susie, we need not talk at all, our eyes would whisper for us, and your hand fast in mine, we would not ask for language—I try to bring you nearer, I chase the weeks away till they are quite departed, and fancy you have come, and I am on my way through the green lane to meet you, and my heart goes scampering so, that I have much ado to bring it back again, and learn it to be patient, till that dear Susie comes. Three weeks—they cant last always, for surely they must go with their little brothers and sisters to their long home in the west!

I shall grow more and more impatient until that dear day comes, for till now, I have only mourned for you; now I begin to hope for you.

Dear Susie, I have tried hard to think what you would love, of something I might send you—I at last saw my little Violets, they begged me to let them go, so here they are—and with them as Instructor, a bit of knightly grass, who also begged the favor to accompany them—they are but small, Susie, and I fear not fragrant now, but they will speak to you of warm hearts at home, and of the something faithful which "never slumbers nor sleeps"—Keep them 'neath your pillow, Susie, they will make you dream of blue-skies, and home, and the 'blessed contrie'! You and I will have an hour with 'Edward' and 'Ellen Middleton', sometime when you get home—we must find out if some things contained therein are true, and if they are, what you and me are coming to!

Now, farewell, Susie, and Vinnie sends her love, and mother her's, and I add a kiss, shyly, lest there is somebody there! Dont let them see, will you Susie?

Emilie—

Why cant I be the delegate to the great Whig Convention?—dont I know all about Daniel Webster, and the Tariff, and the Law? Then, Susie I could see you, during a pause in the session—but I dont like this country at all, and I shant stay here any longer! 'Delenda est' America, Massachusetts and all!

open me carefully

Lewis Carroll
May Mileham

6 September 1885

7 Lushington Road, Eastbourne

Dearest May,

Thank you very much indeed for the peaches. They were delicious. Eating one was almost as nice as kissing you; Of course not quite; I think, if I had to give the exact measurement, I should say three—quarters as nice; We are having such a lovely time here; and the sands are beautiful. I only wish I could some day come across you, washing your pocket-handkerchief in a pool among the rocks? But I wander on the beach, and look for you, in vain; and then I say, Where is May? And the stupid boatmen reply, 'It isn't May, sir? It's September?' But it doesn't comfort me.

Always your Loving

C.L.D.

Ellen Terry

George Bernard Shaw

It was the 1890s. Ellen Terry was a beautiful and talented actress, and had starred in many plays at the Lyceum Theatre. Having seen her act, Shaw was convinced that she was more fit to act in modern plays, or specifically, his plays.

Shaw and Terry only met once or twice, but their correspondence spanned for years. They often discussed theatre and wrote about getting together, but Terry was with Henry Irving at the time and chose to remain loyal to him.

15 May 1896

Your lovely letters!

I am to blame. Forgive me. My star has stopped dancing, and for a while I am down—down. Just when I was downest, your letter came and comforted sore eyes and sore heart. We sail for home on the 20th. Thanks and ever thanks.

E. T.

Leo Tolstoy

Valeria Arsenev

*Tolstoy and Arsenev were engaged at the time he
wrote the following letter to her, expressing his love.
Though, Tolstoy's private diaries tell a different story
altogether. In them, he has written that he found
Valeria uneducated and frivolous. Unsurprisingly, he
later broke off their engagement and joined the army
instead.*

November 2, 1856

I already love in you your beauty, but I am
only beginning to love in you that which is
eternal and ever previous—your heat, your
soul. Beauty one could get to know and fall
in love with in one hour and cease to love it

as speedily; but the soul one must learn to know. Believe me, nothing on earth is given without labor, even love, the most beautiful and natural of feelings.

Emma Darwin

Charles Darwin

'To wed or not to wed' was the heading of Charles Darwin's list of the pros and cons of marriage. At the age of twenty-nine, he thought about whether he should get married or not. And if yes, to whom? Certainly, she had to be someone he knew well, and cared about. Well then, who better than the woman he had known since he was a child, his first cousin Emma Wedgwood. She was a suitable match. Except for the fact that Emma, a deeply religious woman, was bothered by Charles' lack of faith, their marriage sailed smoothly.

June 1861

I cannot tell you the compassion I have felt for all your sufferings for these weeks past that you have had so many drawbacks. Nor the gratitude I have felt for the cheerful & affectionate looks you have given me when I know you have been miserably uncomfortable.

My heart has often been too full to speak or take any notice I am sure you know I love you well enough to believe that I mind your sufferings nearly as much as I should my own & I find the only relief to my own mind is to take it as from God's hand, & to try to believe that all suffering & illness is meant to help us to exalt our minds & to look forward with hope to a future state. When I see your patience, deep compassion for others self command & above all gratitude for the smallest thing done to help you I cannot help longing that these precious feelings should be offered to Heaven for the sake of your daily happiness. But I find it difficult enough in my own case. I often think of the words "Thou shalt keep him in perfect peace whose mind is stayed on thee." It is feeling & not reasoning that drives one to prayer. I feel presumptuous in writing thus to you.

I feel in my inmost heart your admirable qualities & feelings & all I would hope is that you might direct them upwards, as well as to one who values them above every thing in the world. I shall keep this by me till I feel cheerful & comfortable again about you but it has passed through my mind often lately so I thought I would write it partly to relieve my own mind.

Mark Twain

Olivia Langdon

When Samuel Clemens (Mark Twain was his pen name) had asked for Olivia's hand in marriage, her parents had expressed their apprehension. The wealthy residents who lived in upstate New York did not want a humble journalist for a son-in-law. Eventually they gave in, and Clemens married the love of his life on 2 February 1870, two years after they had first met.

January 2, 1869

My Dearest Livy

I wish I had written you long ago that I was to come here, instead of absurdly forgetting it, for I might have a letter from you to read tonight, just as well as not. I must go without, now, till Monday. How they have abused me in this town, for the last two or three days! But they couldn't get the newspapers to do it. They said there was some mistake, & steadfastly refused—for which I am grateful. The night I should have lectured here, the house was crowded, & yet there was not room for all who came. Tonight it was rainy, slushy & sloppy, & only two-thirds of a house came. They were very cool & did not welcome me to the stage. They were still offended & showed it. But as soon as I saw that, all my distress of mind, all my wavering confidence, all my down-heartedness vanished & I never felt happier or better satisfied on a stage before. And so, within ten minutes we were splendid friends—they unbent, banished their frowns & the affair went off gallantly. A really hearty opposition is inspiring, sometimes. The town dignitaries have called with their congratulations & spent an hour with me & have just gone. The Association are jolly, now, for after all the trouble, they had a better house than usual. But what a pity it was we hadn't the big house that assembled before.

Now I am sitting up again to write, Livy, in disobedience to orders, but then I must—for if I didn't write you wouldn't answer & I never, never, never could enjoy that, you know. And besides, I want to write & so I had rather write & be scolded for it than go to bed & have a good sleep. Even if I only wrote nonsense it would still be pleasant, since it would be chatting with you.

Oh, let me praise you, Livy, & don't take it to heart so. You mustn't deprive me of so harmless a pleasure as that. Even if you prove to me that you have the blemishes you think you have, it cannot appal me any, because with them you will still be better & nobler & lovelier than any woman I have known. I will help you to weed out your faults when you have a harder task before you, which is the helping me to weed out mine. Think of that, Livy—think of that & leave the other to time & circumstances. Now please don't feel hurt when I praise you, Livy, for I know that in so doing I speak only the truth. At last I grant you one fault—& it is self-depreciation.

And isn't it wrong—isn't it showing ingratitude toward the Creator, who has put so little into your nature & your character to find fault with? And yet, after all your self-depreciation is a virtue & a merit, for it comes of the absence of egotism, which is one of the gravest of faults. (It isn't any use. I no sooner accuse you than I hasten to take it back again. It isn't in me to find a fault of any importance in you & believe in it, Livy, & so where is the use in trying? Scold me—scold me hard, dear—& then forgive me.)

I was just delighted with Mr. & Mrs. Langdon's letters—& I saw what an idiot I had been to hurry & apologize for my Christmas letter before they had found any fault with it. But the apology was already gone, & I couldn't stop it. But never mind—I thank them from my heart; & next time I write them I will be sagacious & put a little apology in with the letter. Mr. Langdon speaks of the good policy of my achieving Mrs. L.'s favour "if I ever get permission to come again." Commence on him now Livy! Don't let him get used to harbouring such threating notions as that. Obtain his consent early, and clinch it. If you use proper diligence & enterprise, you can easily make yourself so troublesome that he will be glad to grant it in order to have peace. I could. I saw that Mrs. Langdon's hearty invitation had its effect on Mrs. Fairbanks. She notified me to come & take her to Elmira whenever all circumstances should be favourable (I didn't read your letters to her, Livy— but I suppose I ought to have done it.) She sends her love to all of you, & says she is going to describe how impatient I was for Severance to come, New Year's & how suddenly it died away when your letter came & how serene I looked, in the rocking-chair, with my feet on the mantelpiece, reading it! (I didn't have my feet there, at all——but I looked comfortable, no doubt.)

And you had a delightful philosophy lesson, Livy—& wished that we might study it together some day. It is the echo of a wish that speaks in my heart many & many a time. I think, sometimes, how pleasant it would be to sit, just us two, long winter evenings, & study together, & read favorite authors aloud & comment on them & so imprint them upon our memories. It is so unsatisfactory to read a noble passage & have no one you love, at hand to share the happiness with you. And it is unsatisfactory to read to one's self, anyhow——for the uttered voice so heightens the expression. I think you & I would never tire of reading together. At Mrs. Fairbank's they make selections against my coming, & so I have a great deal of reading aloud to do during my visits.

Scold me all you please, Livy—I love to hear you scold, because you are such an earnest little body. And it does some good, too. But for your scolding I should have written other letters tonight—but now I shall write only this one. You can't imagine how dreadfully wearing this lecturing is, Livy. I begin to be appalled at the idea of doing it another season. I shall try hard to get into the Herald on such terms as will save me from it. If I were to confess how few hours I have slept since I saw you last, you could not easily believe it. But it can't be helped, Livy—it cannot. I have so many visitors, then don't know the circumstances, you know—& the railway trips are very long & tedious—very seldom less than 8 hours. I feel a thousand years old, sometimes. But it don't make so very much difference—I recuperate easily. I thought I was going to sleep, sleep, sleep—& rest, rest, rest—for days, at Mrs. F.'s, & see nobody but the family, & have such a peaceful, quiet, homelike sort of a time, & never go out of the house, for I was very tired—but THEY didn't know, & so I found visits & parties already fixed when I arrived, & so I rushed, day & night without ceasing & made my fatigue infinitely worse. But when it was all done, I told them & so hereafter I am to be at home there, which is to say I am not to drive out, nor walk out, nor visit, nor receive company at all, but am to lead a jolly, rejuvenating, restful life in the very heart of the home circle, & forget that there is a driving, toiling world outside. Then I can come away a new man—a young giant refreshed with new wine—& plunge into business again with vim & energy. Besides, you know, we can have visits & visiting, anywhere—what we want at home is the home folks & nobody else. It will be splendid, won't it, next time?

I thank you for all you say, for everything you say, about religion Livy, & I have as much confidence as yourself that I shall succeed at last, but Oh, it is slow & often discouraging. I am happy in conducting myself rightly—but the emotion, the revealing religious emotion, Livy, will not come, it seems to me. I pray for it—it is all I can do. I know not how to compel an emotion. And I pray every day that you may not be impatient or lose confidence in my final conversion—I pray that you may keep your courage & be of good heart. And I pray that my poisonous & besetting apathy may pass from me. It is hard to be a Christian in spirit, Livy, though the mere letter of the law seems not very difficult as a general thing. I have hope. Send me the Plymouth Pulpits, Livy—I looked for one yesterday, but it did not come.

Goodnight & goodbye. Thank you for the kiss, Livy dear. I send you a dozen herewith! (Livy—Livy—the picture) I love you, Livy. I love you more than I can tell.

Devotedly,
Saml L. C.

Hartford,

November 27, 1875

Livy darling,

Six years have gone by since I made my first great success in life and won you, and thirty years have passed since Providence made preparation for that happy success by sending you into the world.

Every day we live together adds to the security of my confidence that we can never any more wish to be separated than that we can ever imagine a regret that we were ever joined. You are dearer to me today, my child, than you were upon the last anniversary of this birthday; you were dearer then than you were a year before—you have grown more and more dear from the first of those anniversaries, and I do not doubt that this precious progression will continue on to the end.

Let us look forward to the coming anniversaries, with their age and their gray hairs without fear and without depression, trusting and believing that the love we bear each other will be sufficient to make them blessed.

So, with abounding affection for you and our

babies, I hail this day that brings you matronly grace and dignity of three decades!

Always Yours,

S.L.C.

FROM
Oscar Wilde
TO
Constance Wilde

When Oscar Wilde had proposed to Constance, she had said, 'As long as I live, you shall be my lover.' Oscar too, allegedly, felt 'incomplete without her.' They got married in 1884 and had a few good years of marriage . . . until Alfred Douglas entered their lives. Their scandalous love affair ended up destroying their marriage and landed Wilde in jail.

1884

Dear and Beloved

Here and I, and you at the Antipodes. O execrable facts, that keep our lips from kissing, though our souls are one.

What can I tell you by letter? Alas! Nothing that I would tell you. The messages of the gods to each other travel not by pen and ink and indeed your bodily presence here would not make you more you more real: for I feel your fingers in my hair, and you cheek brushing mine. The air is full of the music of your voice, my soul and body seem no longer mine, but mingled in some exquisite ecstasy with yours. I feel incomplete without you.

Ever and ever yours

Oscar

George Bernard Shaw

Ellen Terry

c.1897

The midnight train . . . gets to Dorking at 1 (a.m.) 14th-15th June 1897 . . . stopping just now, but will joggle like mad presently.

Do you read these jogged scrawls, I wonder. I think of your poor eyes, and resolve to tear what I have written up: then I look out at the ghostly country and the beautiful night, and I cannot bring myself to read a miserable book . . . Yes, as you guess, Ellen, I am having a bad attack of you just at present. I am restless; and a man's restlessness always means a woman; and my restlessness means Ellen. And your conduct is often shocking. Today I was wandering somewhere . . . when I glanced at a shop window; and there you were—oh disgraceful and abandoned—in your third Act Sans Gene dress—a mere waistband—laughing wickedly, and saying maliciously: "Look have restless one, at your pillow, at what you are really thinking about." How can you look Window and Grove's camera in the face with such thoughts in your head and almost nothing on . . .

Oh fie, fie, let me get away from this stuff, which you have been listening to all your life, & despise—though indeed, dearest Ellen, these silly longings stir up great waves of tenderness in which there is no guile.

I shall find a letter from you when I get back to Lotus, shall I not? Reigate we are at now; and it's a quarter to one. In ten minutes, Dorking station; in seventeen minutes thereafter, Lotus, and a letter. Only a letter, perhaps not even that. O Ellen, what will you say when the Recording Angel asks you why one of your sins have my name to them?

Oscar Wilde

Lord Alfred Douglas

The famous playwright Oscar Wilde and the son of the Marquis of Queensberry, Lord Alfred Douglas, met in 1891 and dived into a tumultuous love affair. Wilde was married at the time.

The Marquis forbade his son to be with Wilde, threatening to disown him. When Alfred didn't obey, the Marquis paid Wilde a visit. Wilde was called a sodomite. Enraged, Wilde sued Queensberry for criminal libel. The Marquis gave a plea of justification which also mentioned that Wilde had committed sexual acts with men. This evidence was sent to the public prosecutor.

Oscar Wilde was tried for gross indecency and arrested in 1895, the year in which The Importance of Being Earnest *was first performed. His love was deemed a crime and he was sentenced for two years.*

During his lover's imprisonment, Douglas had even written to a magazine that love between men was a 'natural congenital tendency' for people and 'the law has no right to interfere with these people.'

Douglas remained loyal to Wilde throughout his imprisonment. After Wilde's release, they reunited and started living together in Naples.

January of 1893

My Own Boy,

Your sonnet is quite lovely, and it is a marvel that those red rose-leaf lips of yours should be made no less for the madness of music and song than for the madness of kissing. Your slim gilt soul walks between passion and poetry. I know Hyacinthus, whom Apollo loved so madly, was you in Greek days.

Why are you alone in London, and when do you go to Salisbury? Do go there to cool your hands in the grey twilight of Gothic things, and come here whenever you like. It is a lovely place and lacks only you; but go to Salisbury first.

Always, with undying love, yours,

Oscar

March 1893, Savoy Hotel

Dearest of All Boys,

Your letter was delightful, red and yellow wine to me; but I am sad and out of sorts. Bosie, you must not make scenes with me. They kill me, they wreck the loveliness of life. I cannot see you, so Greek and gracious, distorted with passion. I cannot listen to your curved lips saying hideous things to me. I would sooner be blackmailed by every renter in London than to have you bitter, unjust, hating. You are the divine thing I want, the thing of grace and beauty; but I don't know how to do it. Shall I come to Salisbury? My bill here is 49 pounds for a week. I have also got a new sitting room over the Thames. Why are you not here, my dear, my wonderful boy? I fear I must leave; no money, no credit, and a heart of lead.

Your own,

Oscar

Rouen, August 1897

My own Darling Boy,

I got your telegram half an hour ago, and just send a line to say that I feel that my only hope of again doing beautiful work in art is being with you. It was not so in the old days, but now it is different, and you can really recreate in me that energy and sense of joyous power on which art depends.

Everyone is furious with me for going back to you, but they don't understand us. I feel that it is only with you that I can do anything at all. Do remake my ruined life for me, and then our friendship and love will have a different meaning to the world.

I wish that when we met at Rouen we had not parted at all. There are such wide abysses now of space and land between us. But we love each other.

Goodnight, dear.

Ever yours,
Oscar

Pierre Curie

Marie Sklowdowska

"I was struck by the open expression of his face and by the slight suggestion of detachment in his whole attitude. His speech, rather slow and deliberate, his simplicity, and his smile, at once grave and youthful, inspired confidence."

This was what Maria Sklowdowska thought of Pierre Curie when she first met him at Sorbonne University in Paris. Within a year of their meeting, Pierre asked her to marry him. Maria was planning on returning to Poland, but the place where she wanted to work had refused to hire her because she was a woman. She then returned to Paris and married Pierre in 1895. Theirs was a marriage of like minds. They spent their life doing ground-breaking research and sharing a Nobel prize.

August 10, 1894

Nothing could have given me greater pleasure that to get news of you. The prospect of remaining two months without hearing about you had been extremely disagreeable to me: that is to say, your little note was more than welcome.

I hope you are laying up a stock of good air and that you will come back to us in October. As for me, I think I shall not go anywhere; I shall stay in the country, where I spend the whole day in front of my open window or in the garden.

We have promised each other—haven't we?— to be at least great friends. If you will only not change your mind! For there are no promises that are binding; such things cannot be ordered at will. It would be a fine thing, just the same, in which I hardly dare believe, to pass our lives near each other, hypnotized by our dreams: your patriotic dream, our humanitarian dream, and our scientific dream.

Of all those dreams the last is, I believe, the only legitimate one. I mean by that that we are powerless to change the social order and, even if we were not, we should not know what to do; in taking action, no matter in what direction, we should never be sure of not doing more harm than good, by retarding some inevitable evolution. From the scientific point of view, on the contrary, we may hope to do something; the ground is solider here, and any discovery that we may make, however small, will remain acquired knowledge.

See how it works out: it is agreed that we shall be great friends, but if you leave France in a year it would be an altogether too Platonic friendship, that of two creatures who would never see each other again. Wouldn't it be better for you to stay with me? I know that this question angers you, and that you don't want to speak of it again—and then, too, I feel so thoroughly unworthy of you from every point of view.

I thought of asking your permission to meet you by chance in Fribourg. But you are staying there, unless I am mistaken, only one day, and on that day you will of course belong to our friends the Kovalskis.

Believe me your very devoted

Pierre Curie

P.S: I would be quite happy if you would write to me and assure me you will come back in October. If you write to me in Sceaux, the mail reaches me faster: Pierre Curie, 13 rue des Sablons, in Sceaux (Seine).

Edith Wharton

W Morton Fullerton

Morton had gotten out of a brief marriage with a French singer when Henry James first introduced him to Edith Wharton. Edith was hoping to get out of her unfulfilling marriage of twenty years. Their meeting in 1907 led to a friendship and then to a love affair that culminated in Edith moving to Paris in 1908 to be with the love of her life, even if he was infamous for being a womanizer and had a sexual history rivalling Byron's.

April 1910

Don't think I am 'fâchée,' as you said yesterday; but I am sad & bewildered beyond words, & with all my other cares & bewilderments, I can't go on like this!

When I went away I thought I should perhaps hear once from you. But you wrote me every day— you wrote me as you used to three years ago! And you provoked me to answer in the same way, because I could not see for what other purpose you were writing. I thought you wanted me to write what was in my heart!

Then I come back, & not a word, not a sign. You know that here it is impossible to exchange two words, & you come here, & come without even letting me know, so that it was a mere accident that I was at home. You go away, & I seem not to exist for you. I don't understand.

If I could lean on some feeling in you—a good & loyal friendship, if there's nothing else!—then I could go on, bear things, write, & arrange my life . . .

Now, ballottée [tossed] perpetually between one illusion & another by your strange confused conduct of the last six months, I can't any longer find a point de repère [landmark]. I don't know what you want, or what I am! You write to me like a lover, you treat me like a casual acquaintance!

Which are you—what am I?

Casual acquaintance, no; but a friend, yes. I've always told you I foresaw that solution, & accepted it in advance. But a certain consistence of affection is a fundamental part of friendship. One must know á quoi s'en tenir [what to hold on to]. And just as I think we have reached that stage, you revert abruptly to the other relation, & assume that I have noticed no change in you, & that I have not suffered or wondered at it, but have carried on my life in serene insensibility until you chose to enter again suddenly into it.

I have borne all these inconsistencies & incoherences as long as I could, because I love you so much, & because I am so sorry for things in your life that are difficult & wearing—but I have never been capricious or exacting, I have never, I think, added to those difficulties, but have tried to lighten them for you by a frank & faithful friendship. Only now a sense of my worth, & a sense also that I can bear no more, makes me write this to you. Write me no more such letters as you sent me in England.

It is a cruel & capricious amusement.—It was not necessary to hurt me thus! I understand something of life, I judged you long ago, & I accepted you as you are, admiring all your gifts & your great charm, & seeking only to give you the kind of affection that should help you most, & lay the least claim on you in return. But one cannot have all one's passionate tenderness demanded one day, & ignored the next, without reason or explanation, as it has pleased you to do since your enigmatic change in December. I have had a difficult year—but the pain within my pain, the last turn of the screw, has been the impossibility of knowing what you wanted of me, & what you felt for me—at a time when it seemed natural that, if you had any sincere feeling for me, you should see my need of an equable friendship—I don't say love because that is not made to order!—but the kind of tried tenderness that old friends seek in each other in difficult moments of life. My life was better before I knew you. That is, for me, the sad conclusion of this sad year. And it is a bitter thing to say to the one being one has ever loved d'amour.

George Bernard Shaw

Erica Cotterill

Erica Cotterill a.k.a. Miss Charming was a fan of George Bernard Shaw and her letters pleased and amused the object of her desire. Shaw responded to her letters, sometimes flirting, sometimes spurning her. Cotterill, however, was determined to get him. She even moved to stay near Shaw and paid his house a visit once. Instead of finding her love, his wife answered the door.

The aftermath of this debacle was Shaw's wife hollering at him to sever all communication with this strange woman. Shaw did what was asked through the following letter, posing as his wife.

11 October 1910

My dear Miss Cotterill,

I think I had better write to you to explain exactly
why I intentionally shewed you that I strongly
disapproved of your presence in my house, and
that I did not—and do not—intend that your
visit should be repeated. You might easily think
that I was merely annoyed by your coming at an
inconsiderate & unusual hour—as indeed I was—
or that I disliked you. That was not it at all. I should
object to your coming at tea time just as much as
I do not particularly dislike you. On the contrary,
it is because you are in some ways rather fine and
sensitive, so that it is very difficult to be unkind to
you, that I am determined to put a stop at once and
for ever to any personal intimacy between us.

The matter is a very simple one. You have made
a declaration of your feelings to my husband; and
you have followed that up by coming to live near us
with the avowed object of gratifying those feelings
by seeing as much as possible of him. If you were
an older and more experienced woman I should
characterize that in terms which would make any
further acquaintance between us impossible. As you
are young and entirely taken by your own feelings, I

can only tell you that when a woman makes such a declaration to a married man, or a man to a married woman, there is an end of all honourable question of their meeting one another again—intentionally at least. You do not understand this, perhaps; but you will later on, when you are married and know what loyalty men owe one another in that very delicate and difficult relation. The present case is a specially difficult and dangerous one, for my husband is not a common man; if you become at all intimate with him he would become a necessity of life to you; and then the inevitable parting would cost you more suffering that it can now. I could not trust him to keep you at a distance: he is quite friendly and sympathetic with everybody, from dogs and cats to dukes and duchesses, and none of them can imagine that his universal friendliness is not a special regard for them. He has already allowed you to become far more attached to him than he should; and I do not intend to let you drift any further into an impossible situation.

If I must end by saying that this letter does not admit of any argument or reply, and that I do not mean it to lead to any correspondence between us, do not conclude that I am writing you in an unfriendly spirit. It would be no use to discuss the matter now; and later on, when you are married and as old as I am, it will not be necessary. Meanwhile believe that my decision is quite inevitable and irrevocable.

Yours sincerely,
Charlotte F. Shaw

Stella Campbell

George Bernard Shaw

18th November 1912

33 Kensington Square

No more shams—a real love letter this time—then I can breathe freely, and perhaps who knows begin to sit up and get well—

I haven't said 'kiss me' because life is too short for the kiss my heart calls for . . . All your words are as idle wind — Look into my eyes for two minutes without speaking if you dare! Where would be your 54 years? and my grandmother's heart? and how many hours would you be late for dinner?

—If you give me one kiss and you can only kiss me if I say 'kiss me' and I will never say 'kiss me' because I am a respectable widow and I wouldn't let any man kiss me unless I was sure of the wedding ring—

Stella

(Liza, I mean)

George Bernard Shaw

Stella Campbell

The love affair between the playwright George Bernard Shaw and his muse, the actress Beatrice Rose Stella Tanner was known to all in the literary circle. Shaw had fallen for the actress after watching her in a few plays. She was the inspiration behind the character Eliza Doolittle in Shaw's renowned play Pygmalion.

Shaw and Beatrice soon became 'Joey' and 'Stella' for each other, and secretly began exchanging letters. Unsurprisingly, Shaw's wife Charlotte wasn't pleased when she heard about them and did whatever she could to keep them apart. Charlotte's prayers were answered when just before Pygmalion's release, Beatrice married someone else and the wretched affair ended. But even that did not put a dent in their affection for each other and they continued writing to each other till Beatrice's death.

c.1911-1925

Stella, Stella Stella Stella Stella Stella Stella Stel
Stella Stella Stella Stella Stella Stella Stella Stel
Stella Stella Stella Stella Stella Stella Stella Stel
Stella Stella Stella Stella Stella what is there le
to say?

I have just played all sorts of things, almo
accurately, I don't believe I could get a headach
if I tried. I drove from Hatfield faster than a ma
should drive in the dark.

What an enormous meal of happiness! The
will wish you many happy returns of Sunda
Sunday! I laugh hollowly. When I am dead let ther
put an inscription on 12 Hinde St HERE A GREA
MAN FOUND HAPPINESS. Wagner wrote u
on his house Hier womein Wahnen Frieden fan
(Wahnfried sei dieses Haus genannt) (if I recollect
aright). Nobody can translate it; but I understand i
I will write on the sky someday.

I was only twenty minutes late for m
appointment; and if I had been wise enough t
miss it altogether I should have saved $300; for th
is just what keeping it cost me in money. What
cost me in absence three hundred millions coul
not pay for.

Her last words as we parted (very affectionately on my part) were 'I never know where you spend your afternoons. Once I never thought about it—never doubted. Now—I always imagine—' I see you, like the Flying Dutchman, since in seven years; and I am supposed to see you every seven minutes. It is amazing to myself that I don't. How is it that I will get up and trudge through the mud to any sort of miserable work, but that I must always let heaven come to me? I should not have come up today but for that silly committee and two other utterly frivolous businesses. It is incredible. How did I get it ground into me that happiness is always picked up on the way and must not be sought? Yet there is something in it: it came nobly off today. Stella: I WAS happy. Was! I am. I shall never be unhappy again.

You cannot have this in the morning because the evening post, at six, had gone before I returned; so this must wait until morning and will reach you in the afternoon—oh Stella Stella Stella Stella Stella Stella

G.B.S

Katherine Mansfield
John Middleton Murry

John Murry met Katherine Mansfield when he was a scholar at Brasenose College, Oxford. Katherine was a woman known as much for her writing as for her sexual ambiguity. She had had a string of lovers before Murry.

Shortly after knowing Katherine, Murry moved into her flat, which she shared with another roommate. Only a lodger at the time, he soon became her lover. They got married to each other once Katherine's divorce with her first husband had been finalized. They were together for eleven years, till Katherine's death in 1923.

Saturday Night

May 18, 1917

My darling,

Do not imagine, because you find these lines in your private book that I have been trespassing. You know I have not—and where else shall I leave a love letter? For I long to write you a love letter tonight. You are all about me—I seem to breathe you—hear you—feel you in me and of me—What am I doing here? You are away—I have seen you in the train, at the station.

When you came to tea this afternoon you took a brioche broke it in half & padded the inside doughy bit with two fingers. You always do that with a bun or roll or a piece of bread.—It is your way—your head a little on one side the while . . .

When you opened your suitcase, I saw your old Feltie & a French book and a comb all higgledy-piggledy. "Tig, I've only got three handkerchiefs." Why should that memory be so sweet to me? . . .

Last night, there was a moment before you got into bed. You stood, quite naked, bending forward a little—talking. It was only for an instant. I saw you—I loved you so—loved your body with such tenderness. Ah, my dear! And I am not thinking now of 'passion'. No, of that other thing that makes me feel that every inch of you is so precious to me—your soft shoulders—your creamy warm skin, your ears, cold like shells are cold—your long legs & your feet that I love to clasp with my feet—the feeling of your belly—& your thin young back. Just below that bone that sticks out at the back of your neck you have a little mole. It is partly because we are young that I feel this tenderness—I love your youth—I could not bear that it should be touched even by a cold wind if I were the Lord.

We two, you know, have everything before us, and we shall do very great things—I have perfect faith in us—and so perfect is my love for you that I am, as it were, still, silent to my very soul. I want nobody but you for my lover and my friend and to nobody but you shall I be faithful.

I am yours forever.

Tig.

Zelda Fitzgerald

F Scott Fitzgerald

The clever, independent, and free-spirited, Zelda Sayre and charming, handsome Scott Fitzgerald met in 1918 at Montgomery Country Club. Thus began a passionate love affair but Zelda had broken off with Scott once, unsure of his financial situation. When The Side of Paradise *was published—Scott's first novel—it was an instant bestseller. Zelda promptly agreed to marry him after this.*

Spring 1919

Sweetheart,

Please, please don't be so depressed—We'll be married soon, and then these lonesome nights will be over forever—and until we are, I am loving, loving every tiny minute of the day and night— Maybe you won't understand this, but sometimes when I miss you most, it's hardest to write—and you always know when I make myself—Just the ache of it all—and I can't tell you. If we were together, you'd feel how strong it is—you're so sweet when you're melancholy. I love your sad tenderness—when I've hurt you—That's one of the reasons I could never be sorry for our quarrels—and they bothered you so—Those dear, dear little fusses, when I always tried so hard to make you kiss and forget—

Scott—there's nothing in all the world I want but you—and your precious love—All the material things are nothing. I'd just hate to live a sordid, colorless existence—because you'd soon love me less—and less—and I'd do anything—anything— to keep your heart for my own—I don't want to live—I want to love first, and live incidentally— Why don't you feel that I'm waiting—I'll come to you, Lover, when you're ready—Don't don't ever think of the things you can't give me—You've trusted me with the dearest heart of all—and it's so damn much more than anybody else in all the world has ever had—

How can you think deliberately of life without me—If you should die—O Darling—darling

Scott—It'd be like going blind. I know I would, too,—I'd have no purpose in life—just a pretty—decoration. Don't you think I was made for you? I feel like you had me ordered—and I was delivered to you—to be worn—I want you to wear me, like a watch—charm or a button hole bouquet—to the world. And then, when we're alone, I want to help—to know that you can't do anything without me.

I'm glad you wrote Mamma. It was such a nice sincere letter—and mine to St. Paul was very evasive and rambling. I've never, in all my life, been able to say anything to people older than me—Somehow I just instinctively avoid personal things with them—even my family. Kids are so much nicer.

F Scott Fitzgerald

Isabelle Amorous

1920

No personality as strong as Zelda's could go
without getting criticisms and as you say she
is not above reproach. I've always known that.
Any girl who gets stewed in public, who frankly
enjoys and tells shocking stories, who smokes
constantly and makes the remark that she has
'kissed thousands of men and intends to kiss
thousands more', cannot be considered beyond
reproach even if above it.

But, Isabelle, I fell in love with her courage,
her sincerity and her flaming self respect and
it's these things I'd believe in even if the whole

world indulged in wild suspicions that she wasn't all that she should be.

But of course the real reason, Isabelle, is that I love her and that's the beginning and end of everything. You're still a Catholic but Zelda's the only God I have left now.

Vita Sackville-West

Virginia Woolf

Vita Sackville-West's love affair with the famous writer Virginia Woolf was the talk of the town in their time. They first met in 1922 at a dinner party hosted by Woolf's brother-in-law, Clive Bell. From there blossomed love between the two women. Vita was head over heels in love with Virginia and for Virginia, Vita was not only her lover but also her muse.

The fact that both Vita and Virginia were married never became an obstruction. Leonard Woolf just wanted his wife to be happy, and Vita was in an open marriage.

Milan

Thursday, January 21, 1926

I am reduced to a thing that wants Virginia. I
composed a beautiful letter to you in the sleepless
nightmare hours of the night, and it has all gone: I
just miss you, in a quite simple desperate human way.
You, with all your un-dumb letters, would never write
so elementary a phrase as that; perhaps you wouldn't
even feel it. And yet I believe you'll be sensible of a
little gap. But you'd clothe it in so exquisite a phrase
that it would lose a little of its reality. Whereas with
me it is quite stark: I miss you even more than I could
have believed; and I was prepared to miss you a good
deal. So this letter is just really a squeal of pain. It is
incredible how essential to me you have become. I
suppose you are accustomed to people saying these
things. Damn you, spoilt creature; I shan't make you
love me any the more by giving myself away like
this—But oh my dear, I can't be clever and stand-
offish with you: I love you too much for that. Too
truly. You have no idea how stand-offish I can be
with people I don't love. I have brought it to a fine
art. But you have broken down my defences. And I
don't really resent it.

However I won't bore you with any more.

We have re-started, and the train is shaky again. I shall have to write at the stations—which are fortunately many across the Lombard plain.

Venice. The stations were many, but I didn't bargain for the Orient Express not stopping at them. And here we are at Venice for ten minutes only,—a wretched time in which to try and write. No time to buy an Italian stamp even, so this will have to go from Trieste.

The waterfalls in Switzerland were frozen into solid iridescent curtains of ice, hanging over the rock; so lovely. And Italy all blanketed in snow.

We're going to start again. I shall have to wait till Trieste tomorrow morning. Please forgive me for writing such a miserable letter.

V.

Virginia Woolf

Vita Sackville-West

7 October 1928

Dearest Creature

It was a very very nice letter you wrote by the light of the stars at midnight. Always write then, for your heart requires moonlight to deliquesce it. And mine is fried in gaslight, as it is only nine o'clock and I must go to be at eleven. And so I shant say anything: not a word of the balm to my anguish—for I am always anguished—that you were to me. How I watched you! How I felt—now what was it like? Well, somewhere I have seen a little ball kept bubbling up and down on the spray of a fountain: the fountain is you; the ball me. It is a sensation I get only from you. It is physically stimulating, restful at the same time . . .

Berg